The Dimension Chronicle

Book One

The

CLAIMED

By D.E. Partridge

Contents

1. An Unwanted Orphan

Grace looked around the moonlit room. The orphanage was silent, but outside, the streets of Manhattan were clamorous, despite the fact that it was almost midnight.

Gracine, more often called Grace, had no friends, for the simple reason that there was no one else her age at the orphanage. All of the other thirteen-year-olds had long since been adopted. Not Grace. Strangely, it was like people did not even see that she was there.

I wonder what my parents were like, imagined Grace, not for the first time. *I bet one of them had dark hair and eyes, like me. And one of them probably had my pale skin.* She had been told that her parents had not wanted her. When they had left her at the orphanage, she had been told that they had not looked back. But surely that was not true. Surely they had not just abandoned her?

Grace lay down, blinking up at the crack in the ceiling, trying to keep herself from crying. *Try to think positive,* she reminded herself. *At least it's not raining; then this crack would turn into an awful leak. And tomorrow's Sunday—we will get to go to chapel. That's always good.*

She rolled over, facing away from the window. Eventually, the dull sounds from the street drowned out her thoughts and she fell asleep.

***

The morning was like all the other Sunday mornings that Grace remembered. She climbed out of bed, brushed her teeth and hair, ate breakfast, and re-brushed her teeth. She walked quietly to church with the ten other orphans, Mrs. Black (who owned the orphanage), and her daughter, Nellie. They were a quiet party as they marched in their clean, dull uniforms.

At noon, they ate their dinner in continued silence. Afterwards, they went back to church for the afternoon service. In the evening, the orphans went to bed.

That was the most exciting day of the week.

On weekdays, there was school. Grace was in the seventh grade, but soon she would be in the eighth, then ninth. The only way Grace could imagine herself getting a good job was for her to do well in school and get a college scholarship. Besides, school distracted her from thinking too much about other matters. Grace did not know what she wanted to do when she grew up. Still, she had time.

On Wednesday, a lady came to the orphanage. She did not want to see the eleven older orphans, but instead she looked at the babies, of which there were nine. After she left at noon, the older children sighed. No one wanted *them.*

Friday brought another couple. They loved little Adeline, who was five. They left with her. They would foster her until they finished the adoption process.

Grace frowned and gripped her pencil hard as she worked out her math problem. They would *foster* her. Mrs. Black thought it was ironically funny for that to be Grace's last name. *Gracine Foster, 13 years old, orphan. Might sector: CLAIMED. 2nd to T.M.* The words flashed through Grace's head so quickly that she lost track of the math problem. *Bother,* she thought. *I guess I have to start over.*

She had no idea where the words came from, or why they had just come into her mind.

But far away in Tennessee, a small woman with auburn hair and piercing green eyes gave a short cry of victory. She had located the first.

Grace was wanted at last.

2. Jerra

Sunday came and went. The end of the school year was fast approaching. Adeline had left the orphanage this year and Johnathan had come. Those were the only differences in the group of children since this time last year.

Except that many of them had grown more bitter and full of hatred. They had gotten more skinny and pitiful—not because they were underfed but because they were under loved.

Nellie was going to college next fall. Grace loved Nellie dearer than anyone else. Nellie was the closest thing to a friend that Grace had. And Nellie would not see Grace again, probably ever.

Grace turned the page of her history book. *From 1560 to 1650, Europe was full of crises in economics and politics. The prices of goods were rising dramatically—* Grace slammed the book shut.

She heard the door open downstairs. Someone had entered the orphanage. The books of the children around Grace slammed shut, too. Everyone sat up straight and listened.

They heard Mrs. Black's heavy footsteps pounding toward the orphanage entryway. They heard voices, but they could not tell what was being said. Mrs. Black gave a shout of surprise. They heard footsteps coming up the stairs. All of the orphans quickly opened their books, pretending they had been studying.

Mrs. Black entered the room. "Gracine Foster! There is someone here who wants to see you. Come along, please."

Grace's head snapped up. "Me?"

"Yes, you! Are there any other Gracine Fosters around here?"

"No, ma'am." Grace quickly stood up and followed Mrs. Black back to the entryway.

The stranger was a young woman, probably about twenty-five. She had dark auburn hair, fair skin, and very pale, piercing green eyes. She looked excited but also impatient.

"Well?" she asked. "Are you Grace Maryanne Foster, daughter of James and Sarabeth Foster?"

Grace gasped. "Do you know who my parents are?"

"Of course! So you *are* Grace Foster, am I correct?"

"Yes, ma'am. Yes, I am," Grace responded.

"Well! This *is* a discovery." The stranger turned to Mrs. Black. "If you could excuse us, please." Mrs. Black nodded and backed out of the room. The stranger continued, "Let me see your right hand, child."

"My—hand?" queried Grace.

"Em-hmm." Grace cautiously extended it. The stranger brushed the back of Grace's hand with her own right hand.

Grace yelped. As soon as they touched, a spark of electricity seemed to race up her arm and into her brain. It made her arm tingle and her ears buzz. After a moment had passed, the buzzing stopped, but her mind seemed more alert—it sizzled with alertness.

"What is this?" cried Grace.

"A test. To see if you are who I thought you are," explained the stranger.

"Am I?"

"I would say so! Here, put these in." The stranger handed a small box to Grace.

"What?" asked Grace.

"Dark contacts. Another effect of the test is that your eyes are now—well, green. When we leave you can take them out, but for now it would be safer."

Grace accomplished this without much trouble. One of the other orphans wore contacts, and Grace had seen her put them in.

"Well, now we leave," announced the stranger.

"What? But what will Mrs. Black think?"

The stranger looked Grace in the eyes. "Everyone here has now forgotten that you ever existed."

"What? No, I don't believe you. Nellie will remember. You can't make Nellie forget!" cried Grace.

"Keep your voice down, child. It is best."

"No one else's new parents did this, you know," Grace challenged. "No one else's new parents *could* do this. That is, if you are not lying. Who are you?"

"Jeraldine Baker. People call me Jerra, though. But enough of that. We should be going, you know." Jerra seized Grace's hand and pulled her toward the door.

"You can't just take me! That's kidnapping! Go away, and leave me here."

"You don't want to go?" Jerra frowned. "I am not trying to force you, but—what is there here for you?"

Grace took a deep breath. "Fine. But where are we going?"

"This way!" said Jerra. She dodged the people in the crowd. Grace took off after her.

When they finally came to a stop after about an hour, they were on an empty alleyway about four miles from the orphanage. Jerra turned to Grace suddenly. "Do you believe in Magic?"

"Do I—believe—in Magic?" panted Grace. "Why does it matter?"

"Because I'm a Magician. And you, my friend, have the ability to become one of the most powerful Magicians Americaea has ever known."

Grace snorted. "Americaea? I don't believe a word you say. Prove it! Prove you're a Magician."

"I will prove it, but Grace, there will be no going back after that. You will not ever be able to go back to your lonely place in that orphanage, no matter how scared or frustrated you get. Do you still want me to prove it, or do you want to go back?"

Grace stared at her. Jerra was serious. The newly awakened part of Grace's mind said, *This could be your only chance to escape the orphanage. If Magicians are real—and if you can be one—is that not so much better than sitting doing sums and learning dates?* Grace frowned but took a step towards Jerra. There was nothing at the orphanage for Grace, as Jerra had pointed out.

"I believe you," Grace announced. "Show me the way."

Jerra took Grace's hand. "Very well—brace yourself." Jerra whispered something inaudible.

They disappeared.

3. The School of the CLAIMED

Grace felt a jolt. If she had not been expecting it, she would have fallen down. The world turned a hazy gray for about five seconds. Then, with another jolt that did knock Grace down, she reappeared in an identical alleyway.

Jerra helped Grace up. "Are you alright? I would have warned you, but it's impossible to speak in between Dimensions."

"What?"

"I suppose you don't know about that yet. All in good time, though, all in good time. Isn't it nice to be home?"

Grace looked up and down the alleyway. "Are we going anywhere? I don't know my way around New York that well, so you ought to lead, Jerra."

"New Yorin, not New York. We're in the Magic Dimension now." Jerra pulled Grace out of the alleyway and onto the sidewalk. "See? Hubert's Potions; Antique Magical Instruments—Wands, Cauldrons, and so much more!; Classical Telescopes for the Modern Observer; and look!— Charms, Spells, and Enchantments on Necklaces, Rings, and Bracelets. In Normality you call them charms, but here they actually *are* Charms, you see."

"Ah," said Grace, who did not have the least idea what Jerra was talking about.

"And there's Storing Stones—they went out of business, because, you see, that is just too dangerous. Now, we don't need Shoppes Street, we need School Street. Here we are. So many schools; you wouldn't think we'd need so many. The School of Classical Magic, Willow Wand School for Magicians, Basic Magic for the Young (that's like a Normal preschool), White Magic School, and, of course, the School of the CLAIMED."

"CLAIMED—last Friday, I don't know why, a bunch of words went through my head. My name, my age, the fact that I was an orphan. And then: *Might Sector: CLAIMED. 2nd to T.M.* What does that mean?"

"It means you're CLAIMED—more powerful in Magic than most people." The bitterness in Jerra's voice surprised Grace, but it disappeared in an instant. "But 2nd to T.M? Honestly, I have no idea. But you thought all of those words because I located you—by Magic. We've been trying to find you for a while. The CLAIMED Master did an Enchantment on you that kept someone from adopting you."

Before Grace could ask any more questions, Jerra said, "Well, here you are. The School of the CLAIMED. You will be happy here. Anyway, go in. I've delivered you, so I'd best be getting home now."

Grace turned to the School, which appeared was a dark stone building. It looked utterly untenable. "Jerra?" asked Grace. She turned back to her companion.

But Jerra was gone. Grace had no choice but to go on.

She walked up to the door. There was no knob, no handle of any sort. Grace raised her hand to knock and the door swung open on its own.

"Greetings, Gracine Foster," said a harsh voice. Grace looked up. Seated at one end of the room in a large black chair was a woman with the cruelest, least compassionate face Grace had ever seen. In front of her were two children, one a boy and one a girl, who both looked petrified.

"Well! Come in!" snapped the woman. She clapped her hands and the door closed behind Grace. "Last room to the right is yours. Get a move on!" For the first time Grace noticed that the hall was lined with doors—five on each side. She hurried toward the last door. Like the front door, it swung open before her and closed after her.

The room was small. On the floor lay a dusty mattress. In one corner was the door to a small closet and in another corner sat a rusty metal wash basin. *I guess this is my room,* thought Grace. *It's not too cheery, but—oh! That woman—do I have to live with that woman? I wish I were back at the orphanage.* Grace sat down on the mattress with her head in her hands.

At that moment, the door of Grace's room opened. Grace looked up.

A woman was standing in the doorway, and she was not the one who had been teaching the children. This lady had light, shiny blonde hair, flashing green eyes, and a blue dress that seemed to blow about her of its own accord. "Oh, dear." Her voice was soft and gentle—*silvery,* Grace noted. "May I come in?" The woman asked.

Grace nodded. The woman seemed pleased by this. "You can take out the contacts now, dear." She smiled at Grace, and Grace blinked. She had forgotten about that.

"Who was that—person—in there?" questioned Grace, while she hurriedly removed the contacts from her eyes.

"Oh, yes. Whenever I am not able to be here—which is not frequent, but it does happen—she comes and teaches the children. For lack of a better word, she is the *substitute teacher*. She is not CLAIMED, whereas I am, therefore I am more qualified for the role of teacher. I don't understand why she likes to keep things in this condition." The woman snapped her fingers. The bed that Grace was sitting on instantly cleaned itself off while seeming to jump into the air. Grace had to grab it to keep from being flung across the room like a leaf in the wind. As she relaxed her grip on the bed she noticed that the room was now sparklingly clean.

She glanced down at the bed again and stared. It was now magnificent. It had a splendid wooden headboard full of curls, twists, and turns. The basin, too, had changed. Over it towered a large and beautiful mirror, below it was a neatly carved stand for the basin to sit upon, and the basin itself was now made out of white porcelain. Painted on it were lovely images of flowers and bluebirds.

Best of all, the walls and floor were no longer dark stone. They were marble, and a soft carpet lay upon the floor.

"That is much better," stated the woman. "You ought to come meet the others now. There are two other young CLAIMED here. You will also be surprised to see the hall, Grace." There was fun sparkling in the woman's bright eyes.

"Yes, ma'am," Grace said, standing. "But you did not tell me your name."

"I am called the CLAIMED Master. Not because I am my students' master but because I am a Master of Magic. It is an old title. Come along."

"Yes, Master." Grace smiled up at the Master, and the Master smiled back.

They entered the hall. Grace gasped. The hall was now constructed of marble. Lined up on the center of the ceiling were five chandeliers, each in a row with two of the ten doors. The chandeliers glowed with the light of many candles, casting startlingly bright light and starkly contrasting shadows over the whole hall. At the end of the room, where the black chair had been, now sat a white chair. It was larger than the black one, and heaped upon it were multiple cushions and pillows. Above it was an enormous window facing the west. The sun was setting, and the light made the curtain framing the window glow, shining a pale spotlight on the chair underneath it.

"Is that better, do you think?" queried the Master.

"Better? Oh, it's beautiful, just beautiful. It's like a castle!" exclaimed Grace.

The Master laughed. "I am glad you share my taste in decoration. Besides, it is easier to work in a properly lit space." She paused for a moment in thought. Then she gestured to another door, on the same side of the hall as Grace's own, but closer to the door that went outside. It was the door second-closest to the entry door. "Go in there," the Master instructed. "That is Andrea's room."

Grace nodded and approached the indicated door. As the others had, it swung open before her. "Hello?" she called cautiously. "Is anyone there?"

A face appeared at the door. It was lightly tanned with a few freckles scattered across the nose. The girl's hair hung behind her in long, sandy, blond waves. "Oh, hello! I thought you might come by soon. The Master was not glad you came on the day Sub was teaching. She is not always the warmest welcome. But you came today!"

Grace nodded.

"Anyway," continued the girl. "Come right on in. Make yourself at home. My name's Andrea Burlington."

"Oh… okay," said Grace, stepping into the room. The furniture was identical to Grace's, but Andrea had definitely personalized the room. On one wall was a picture of Andrea with the boy who had been in the hall earlier and two adults who the children resembled. On another wall was a bulletin board upon which was pinned multiple pieces of paper. "What are those?" asked Grace, pointing.

"My notes. See—" Andrea raised her hand and one of the pieces of paper flew into it. She handed it to Grace. The paper read:

To uncloak, unbind,

And thus find: Revealius!

"It's a simple Charm—they learn this at the Basic Magic School. See, I took this note when I was six—eight years ago."

"You're fourteen?" Grace questioned.

"Yes—as of a month ago," answered Andrea.

The door opened again. Both girls turned to see who had entered the room. It was the boy from earlier. His piercing green eyes shone out from his lightly tanned face, starkly contrasting his sandy-blond hair. Andrea raised her hand back towards the bulletin board and the note neatly pinned itself back in place. She then turned to face her twin brother.

"Hi, Andy," the boy winked at Andrea. He saw Grace and smiled mischievously. "Hi, I'm Tom. Or, if you want to be specific—" he grinned at his sister. She rolled her eyes. "—I'm Thomas George Sylvester Joseph Kean Burlington. And she's Andrea Syb—"

A spark of alarm instantly entered Andrea's eyes. "Don't, Tom! Remember?"

"She's Andrea Sybil Lydia Sarabeth Foster Burlington." Andrea winced at his conclusion.

"What?" cried Grace. "Wait, Sarabeth Foster—that was my mother's name!"

Andrea gave Tom a pointed glare. He looked down, ashamed. "Oops," he muttered.

"Why do you have my mother's name?" asked Grace curiously.

"Our mom was friends with your mom," Andrea explained, blinking furiously. This was not one of her favorite topics of discussion.

Grace's eyes widened. "Your parents knew my parents? Like, actually, *knew* my parents?"

Andrea looked at her. "I don't want to talk about this, okay? It's just…" She shrugged.

Grace turned to Tom, desperate for him to tell her. "You know the truth. What is it? Why does your sister have my mom's name?"

Andrea glared at Tom. Tom ran from the room. Grace frowned. "Fine," she growled. She reached for her newly discovered Magical power. If Andrea would not talk, Grace would make her talk. She willed Andrea to levitate. Maybe if Andrea was scared she would tell Grace her secret. Instead of hovering in the air, Andrea was lifted bodily and thrown on the bed. Grace gasped and ran over, horrified at what she had done.

Andrea sat up and stared at Grace. "Are you sure you've never done Magic before—at all?"

"No, I've never." Grace was still curious but was relieved to see Andrea was alright.

"Do you have any idea what you just did? Instantary Willful Levitation—I have never done that, ever! It will be interesting to know you, I believe."

Grace frowned but decided to give up her search for information—for the moment, at least. "It wasn't anything. I can't, like, take people between Dimensions, or anything."

"Oh, that. Most people have the ability to do it, but you have to have a license. Jerra Baker is one of the few in Americaea who goes between Dimensions regularly."

"Oh."

"You know what? I believe it is dinner time. Come on, you'll find this interesting."

"What about dinner is so interesting?" asked Grace.

"You just wait and see," smiled Andrea.

4. A Talk with the Master

Grace followed Andrea into the hall. With a mischievous grin, Andrea pushed Grace into the center of the room, and then Andrea stepped back.

The Master strode forward and clapped her hands twice. She whispered something inaudible. The section of the floor upon which Grace stood shot three feet upwards and unfolded its legs. It now formed a table. Grace stumbled, so Andrea caught her as she fell and set her upright on her feet. "That's payback for throwing me earlier," whispered Andrea, grinning.

Grace just smiled. On each side of the table four chairs had sprung up, as well as one at each end. "I agree," Grace responded. "Interesting."

"Oh, it's just starting," warned Andrea.

She was right. A plate fell from the ceiling onto the table at each place, but none of them cracked, despite being made of the finest porcelain. A moment later, a packet fell on top of each plate. Grace raised her eyebrows questioningly at Andrea.

"You'll see," whispered Andrea.

"Seat yourselves, children," instructed the Master. The children obeyed. "Welcome, Grace," continued the Master. "Andrea, show our new student how dinner works here, please."

Andrea nodded. She glared at the packet on the table. "Eat a treat: Squash casserole." The package, much to Grace's astonishment, neatly unwrapped itself, and there on

17

Andrea's plate was a miniature version of squash casserole. "Grow," commanded Andrea. The squash casserole immediately obliged—its size increasing rapidly until Andrea commanded, "Stop." On her plate was a steaming, delicious smelling plate of her desired meal: squash casserole.

"Enchanting," breathed Grace.

"Nay," corrected the Master. "Merely Charming. Alright, your turn, Thomas."

Tom nodded. "Eat a treat: Fried chicken! Grow." He paused. Grace grinned at the thought of *fried chicken* here, of all things. "Stop!" commanded Tom.

Grace choked with contained laughter. "Fried chicken?" she queried.

The Master turned to her. "The Dimensions are parallel. If a significant event happens in one, it has to happen it the other. You would be surprised how different history would have been without the invention of fried chicken." She paused, allowing this to soak in. "Now, Grace, it is your turn. Remember: the first rule of Magic is that matter can neither be created nor destroyed. Therefore, the miniature version is extremely dense, whereas the larger version is perfect. If you let it grow too long, however, your meal will be filled with air bubbles and gaps. Now, try."

Grace thought a moment. "Eat a treat: Tomato soup. Grow." She concentrated. "Stop!" In front of her sat a steaming bowl of soup.

"Very nice," complimented the Master. "You might be surprised to learn how many people forget to specify which *kind* of soup. That is quite a mess! They get a bit of tomato soup, a bit of potato soup, some shrimp, some chicken, occasionally some beef, and typically a good amount of spinach. Ugh!" She made a face before turning to her own package. "Eat a treat: Okra salad. Grow." She paused. "Stop," she completed. The group began to eat.

After a few bites Andrea spoke. "You know, Grace did Instantary Willful Levitation earlier."

The Master nodded in approval. "Very good. A wonderful beginning—very promising indeed."

Andrea continued, "With *me*."

The Master looked up sharply. She studied Grace with raised eyebrows. "I see." She spoke quietly, calculatingly. "Grace—before Jerra found you, did any unexpected words go through your head?"

"Um—yes." Grace felt uncomfortable.

"Tell me what they were," commanded the Master.

Grace looked at her, puzzled. "Gracine Maryanne Foster, 13 years old, orphan. Might sector: CLAIMED. 2nd to T.M."

The Master stood, pushing her chair back. "Tom, Andrea, finish your dinner and entertain yourselves. Grace, you come with me." The Master strode towards the door opposite Grace's. The door, as always, opened itself.

"Am I in trouble?" asked Grace.

The Master stopped and turned around. "Oh, no. I'm sorry. No, you're not. I just want to talk to you."

Grace nodded and glanced around the room. On one wall was a window to the south. It showcased the dark night sky out over New Yorin, with a brilliant display of stars unobscured by pollution. The floor, unlike Grace's, appeared to be wooden, and the walls were painted white, not marble.

"My room," announced the Master. "Simpler than the others, but just how I want it." She dug into a bunch of papers which were sitting on her desk. Finally, she extended her hand and one of the papers flew into it from the bottom of the pile. "Well!" the Master exclaimed, quickly enclosing it in her hand. She turned to Grace and gestured towards the bed. "Sit down." Grace obeyed. "Now," the Master continued. "Do you have any questions?"

Grace frowned at her. "Do I have any questions?"

The Master smiled. "I suppose I should have asked, 'What is your *first* question?'"

"Okay—what are the Dimensions?"

"That is a great place to start. This Dimension, as you may have already guessed, is the Magic Dimension. You came from the Normal Dimension, or the Dimension of Normality. There are two other Dimensions—Good and Evil—but those are less parallel than Magic and Normality. But now! I'm getting ahead of myself. Each of the Dimensions—ordinary and extraordinary—balance each other out. Things in one Dimension are parallel to things in another. For example, we are currently in New Yorin, but in Normality this city is called—"

"New York!" finished Grace triumphantly.

"Correct. It is also in the same place geographically. And there are parallel cities in Good and Evil as well, although it is impossible to get to those Dimensions."

"So—it's like four parallel universes?" observed Grace.

"Precisely," the Master confirmed.

"Okay," Grace moved on to her next topic of choice. "What does CLAIMED mean? I've heard that word a million times today, but no one has given any explanation."

"That," began the Master, "is a less specific question. The title CLAIMED originated several hundred years ago with a Magician who was known as the True Master. He wrought several powerful Enchantments during his lifetime. Eventually he used up too much of his power at once and he died. We do know, however, that one of his many Enchantments had to do with the CLAIMED. The Enchantment chose the most powerful Magicians and CLAIMED them for a certain destiny. Those who are chosen cannot thwart it; it was, after all, created by the most powerful Magician ever."

"But what is the destiny?" inquired Grace.

"That is a question for another time," replied the Master gently.

Grace nodded. "Alright..." She looked up, calculating how much the Master would be willing to tell her. The question had, after all, affected Andrea very strongly earlier. "Why does Andrea have my mother's name?"

"Oh, child." The Master frowned. "I should not be the one to tell you that story. Ask Andrea or Tom later."

"I have. They refused."

"I see. Well..." the Master began. "Your parents were...how do I put this...being *hunted* by someone— someone who wanted to kill them. The same was true for the parents of Andrea and Thomas Burlington. Your mother and theirs were the best and closest of friends. When both of them knew they were pregnant, they decided to keep you and the twins apart, hoping that by doing this they would be keeping you safe. The Burlingtons brought Tom and Andrea here and put them under my care, and your parents took you to another Dimension.

"Your parents chose not to stay with you, believing that their presence would attract their enemies not only to your existence but also to your location. Your parents gave instructions to bring you here when you had grown, but they did not give us your location. When your parents re-entered this Dimension after leaving you, they were surprised by their enemy, and they died. The Burlingtons were devastated that they had not been able to help their dear friends. They mourned in hiding for several years, coming out of their small house on occasion to visit their growing children, whom they now knew were CLAIMED. Eventually, they could hide no longer and they, too, were killed by their enemy.

"You understand now why Andrea has your mother's name—the Burlingtons named their children after their closest friends."

Grace sat stone-faced in horror. It was no wonder that Andrea had not wanted to tell her all of this. "Oh. I see. But—I am glad to know my parents did care for me."

The Master nodded sadly. "Very much," she agreed.

"Were my parents—and the twin's parents—were they CLAIMED?"

"No, Grace. Technically, that would be impossible, because of all the Enchantments surrounding the CLAIMED.

A CLAIMED person cannot do anything that will keep them from their destiny—including getting married. However, all Enchantments are not without glitches." The Master stopped speaking, and her eyes took on a gloomy expression.

Grace failed to notice this. "I can't *ever* get married?"

The Master shook her head. "There is only one way that would possibly happen—if the main objective of the CLAIMED were to be fulfilled, then the Enchantments would disappear."

"And you won't tell me what this objective—this destiny—is?"

"Later, Grace. There are other things that are essential for you to learn first." The Master smiled at her.

"Do Andrea and Tom know?" queried Grace.

The Master laughed. "No, they do not know. They do, however, know many things you do not, seeing as they have been studying Magic all of their lives and you are just beginning. This is not, for any reason, an excuse to go levitating either of them, although on other circumstances I am sure they would appreciate the chance to fly.

"Now, despite the fact that I have gladly answered a few of your questions, I have other purposes for suddenly bringing you in here in the middle of dinner. Tell me, again, what you heard when Jerra found you."

"Gracine Maryanne Foster, 13 years old, orphan." Grace winced. "Might sector: CLAIMED. 2nd to T.M."

"That is what I thought. Are you *positive* you remember correctly?"

Grace nodded. "Absolutely."

The Master frowned. "That is quite—*interesting.* That little phrase '2nd to T.M.' is quite bizarre. If Jerra's Magic had worked as expected, then it would have stopped after 'CLAIMED.' There has not been an addition to the finding phrase *ever.* You are—*unique,* Grace."

"But what does it *mean*?" asked Grace.

"To tell the truth, I honestly don't know for sure. I have some guesses, although the words themselves I have never heard before. It is certainly a Finding Phenomenon. I shall have to think it over." She paused, opening her hand and giving Grace the paper. "In the meantime, I suggest that you study this."

"What is it?" Grace queried curiously.

"Lesson One: The Difference between Charms, Spells, and Enchantments, and The First Rule of Magic. I will work with the twins in the morning and you in the afternoon. I shall expect you to have learned the material and be able to practice."

"Yes—um, okay," Grace responded hesitantly. The parchment in her hand was covered front and back with handwritten script.

The Master smiled kindly. "If you have any questions, please know that this room is always open to you. And now, as it is nearing ten o' clock, you should probably go finish your dinner and head to bed. You will find a nightgown in the closet. Good night, Grace."

"Good night," replied Grace, walking back into the hall. She did as the Master had suggested and went to bed, for she felt exhausted. After all, it had been a long day.

5. To Learn Magic

The morning dawned. For a split second, Grace wondered where she was. Then she remembered. *Oh*, she thought gladly. *It is good to be here.* Slowly, she began to ready herself for the day.

When she finally walked into the hall, the Master was teaching Andrea and Tom, who sat before her with rapt attention. The Master turned to Grace. "I am sorry you missed breakfast. I saved you a biscuit. You will find it in the room to the right of yours. Take Lesson One in there with you to study it." She turned back to Andrea and Tom.

Grace did as the Master had instructed. The biscuit melted in her mouth as she ate, sliding down her throat in a stream of light, fluffy, warm goodness.

Grace looked at the page that she was supposed to be studying. It was written in small, neat handwriting that looped into elegant letters.

Grace began to read. *Lesson One: The Difference between Charms, Spells, and Enchantments and the First Rule of Magic. Part One: Charms. Charms are the easiest form of Magic. They are mostly used in household settings for things such as dinner packets and doors. They are also used to produce Illusions. A Charm is cast by using a simple phrase unique to the desired effect. For example, a simple Revealing Charm is as follows:*

To uncloak, unbind,
And thus find: Revealius!

Grace smiled, remembering Andrea's note. The lesson continued, *While using a Charm, you must keep firmly in your mind your specific goal, because the words in the Charm itself are general. For the Revealing Charm, your specific goal would be what you wanted to find.*

Part Two: Spells. Spells are the second most difficult form of Magic. While Charms have to do with inanimate objects, Spells control individual living things. The larger the animal is, the more difficult the Spell will be. (Note— Humans are an exception to this rule. They are the most difficult to perform a Spell upon, even more than a giraffe or an elephant.)

A Spell is not controlled by a phrase, which makes it harder to direct than a Charm. You simply have to direct the Magical energy with will power. An example of a Spell is Instantary Willful Levitation. This Spell is more difficult on a dog than a rabbit, more difficult on an elephant than a dog, and more difficult on a human than an elephant. Grace glanced up from the paper. Now she understood why the others had been so surprised. She continued to read. *DO NOT try this without a powerful grownup's supervision. If you try too hard it is possible to overexert yourself to the point of death.* Grace crossed her arms. *I didn't mean to,* she thought obstinately.

The page continued. *Part Three: Enchantments. The most advanced Magic is called Enchanting. Enchanting does not cover inanimate objects or singular animals. Instead, Enchantments are a Magical binding of objects to animals or of several animals together. Like Spells, the difficulty varies according to the size of the things upon which the Magic is used, and, once again, people are an exception to the rule, being the most difficult.*

An Enchantment is unique in another way as well. While Charms are controlled solely by words and Spells are controlled solely by will, an Enchantment can be worked using either. The results are easier to control using words, but the power of the Magic is dependent upon the lack of words. Thus a spoken Enchantment is easier but weaker than a willful Enchantment.

Few Enchantments are worked these days because there are a diminishing number of those who are powerful enough to work them. However, one of the greatest Enchantments was used to separate the strongest Magicians from the rest and to give said strong Magicians a specific purpose. This purpose is unknown by most of those who are not part of the chosen group.

Part Four: The First Rule of Magic. The First Rule of Magic is that matter cannot be created or destroyed. If you try to make something grow, its consistency becomes thinner. If you make something shrink, the object becomes denser. An object will have the same weight no matter its size, thus you must be wary of picking something up after a recent Shrinking or Growing.

The most common question regarding this rule is as follows. "If said rule is true, how do people make things such as furniture and other objects appear and disappear at will?" Grace instantly recalled the transformation of the school. *That says, "at will;" it must have been a Spell,* she realized. She continued to read. *The objects do not actually appear or disappear. They are only hidden with a strong*

27

Illusion from all foreseeable angles. If a wall were to be knocked out of a building that was cloaked in an Illusion, a person on the other side would see the building as it really was, not as the Illusion. The reason for this is that the Spell's creator did not foresee that anyone would try to look at the building from that angle. The page ended abruptly.

Oh, my, Grace thought. *Learning Magic might not be that different from learning math after all. Rules of Magic, rules of math—it's really all quite similar. Still, this is interesting. When I put it into practice, it will be fun, too. Judging by yesterday, performing Magic will actually be pretty easy.*

Grace had never been so wrong in her life. When the Master called her in after lunch, Grace sat nervously on the cold stone floor. Instantly, a chair popped up that was similar to but smaller than the Master's.

The Master smiled at her. "Did you have a good morning, Grace?" She asked kindly.

Grace nodded.

"I know it's quite an adjustment for you after being in an orphanage all those years. I am sure you felt bewildered yesterday, and I don't blame you. Do you have any more questions? About yesterday? The lesson? Anything?"

"Is it true—did I perform a Spell yesterday?"

"Oh, yes. A very advanced Spell, actually. I did not expect it, not even from your Discovery. You have a lot of potential, Grace Foster."

Grace spoke up. "A Discovery?" she queried.

"What? Oh, yes. Discovery is one of the most incredible Magical phenomena. When any Magician first becomes aware of his or her potential through what Jerra called 'the test,' he or she attains the ability and knowledge to produce a piece of Magic. Any Magician's first piece of Magic is called their Discovery. A Discovery is considerably higher than their Magical ability at that point in time, but also considerably lower than their Magical ability after a good amount of training."

"So right now I would not be able to lift a human using Magic?" questioned Grace.

"Probably not. However, you have been very unpredictable Magically, so I would not be *as* surprised as I would be if someone else did it. Under normal circumstances, though, no. And, Grace, do not try. Not until I tell you, at least. If you are not strong enough, you *will* die, do you understand me?"

Grace nodded rapidly. "Yes."

"Good," responded the Master. "Any other questions?"

"Is that piece of Magic that transported us between the Dimensions a Charm or a Spell?" asked Grace. "It used words but it had to do with people."

The Master beamed at her. "I am glad you caught that! That particular piece of Magic is actually neither. The rare exceptions to the regular categorization of Magic are called Intermediate pieces of Magic. Intermediate Magic falls in between the Magical categories. It is not a difficult branch of Magic, although you do have to have a license to travel in between Dimensions. Have you noticed that you are not able to talk in between Dimensions?"

"Yes," responded Grace. "Why do you ask?"

"That is because, for the few seconds when you are not in any Dimension, you technically don't exist. It you were to lose hold of the Magic during that time, I don't think you would ever enter a Dimension again. However, this has not been proven because of lack of research. Obviously no one wants to *try* to not exist. Anyway, travelling between the Dimensions is Intermediate Magic."

"What are the words?" Grace queried curiously.

"I am not going to tell you that," announced the Master decidedly. "That information is much too dangerous to reveal without much prior preparation."

"Do the twins know?" asked Grace slyly.

The Master laughed. "Of course not! Do you think I would trust Tom for a minute with that knowledge?" She paused, allowing that to sink in, before she continued. "I suppose you are wondering if I will let you perform some Magic?"

"Yes!" cried Grace eagerly.

"I have decided it would be best. It would be very impractical for you to know the theory of Magic without knowing how to even perform a simple Charm."

"Oh, good." Grace grinned.

"Alright," responded the Master. She bowed her head for a moment in concentration.

Grace blinked, and when she opened her eyes, she discovered that the window had disappeared. She studied the wall for a minute before asking, "From the outside, does it still look like a window?"

"Yes." The Master nodded. "Also, you should notice that it is still providing light to this room. It is not blocked, but instead merely hidden, using one of the simplest Illusion Spells. You can uncover it by using the Revealing Charm in your lesson."

Grace nodded. "And my specific goal is..." She trailed off, glancing at the Master for help.

"Your specific goal should be to find the window," instructed the Master.

"Right," Grace replied. She reached for her newly discovered Magical energy.

"To uncloak, unbind,
And thus find: Revealius!"

she exclaimed, watching in delight as the window popped into sight. She felt slightly winded, as though she had just run a couple laps around the room, but she was not exhausted. Still, she marveled that she had performed a much larger piece of Magic yesterday without being winded at all.

"Good!" cried the Master. "Very, *very* well done. Now, another Charm is

Flight of Might,
Right in sight: Aerobis!

It is a Levitation Charm for small inanimate objects. Here, try it with this." She handed Grace a small glove before continuing. "Set it down and then try to make it fly onto my lap."

Grace obeyed. Carefully, she spoke the words, and the glove soared neatly into the air and onto the Master's lap. Grace felt more winded this time, but not tired.

"Good!" cried the Master again. She continued giving Grace Charms to work until Grace gave a gasp and said, "Please! Can I—rest? I—can't breathe."

The Master frowned. "I am sorry, child. I have gone too far. Go rest, but take Lesson Two with you. And if you want to join us for breakfast tomorrow, I suggest that you rise earlier. Now, go rest."

Grace nodded. She stood slowly with a slight groan and dragged herself to bed.

***

When Grace awoke, she felt mentally stronger, but her body ached as if she had spent all day exercising without taking a single rest. If she looked at it from a Magical perspective, this was not too far from the truth. With a sigh as her body protested, she forced herself to climb out of bed before hurrying into the hall.

The Master, Andrea, and Tom were in the middle of dinner. There was not much true conversation, but Tom was obviously trying to annoy Andrea. He glanced up guiltily as Grace entered the room.

"Greetings, child," the Master smiled at her. "You have slept long. Not that I didn't expect that, of course... But never mind! Come, sit down. You know how to work the dinner packets."

Grace obeyed. Now that she was no longer exhausted, her stomach growled ravenously. She ate hungrily and stared at her plate in dismay after she had emptied it.

The Master laughed, and Grace looked up, bashful. "I think tonight calls for dessert, too," she declared knowingly. Another packet, smaller than the dinner one, fell beside each of their plates.

The children eagerly pushed away their dinners and spoke the dessert Charm. After they finished, they each hurried back to their own rooms and fell asleep.

***

The next morning, Friday, was the same as the previous except that Grace joined Andrea, Tom, and the Master for breakfast before taking her lesson into her room to study. She had set Lesson One on the shelf in her closet for storage. Now she sat on her bed with Lesson Two.

The page read, *Lesson Two: Might Sectors and Magical Keys. Part One: Might Sectors. A Might Sector is the Magical strength of a Magician or wizard. The lowest Sector is a Charmer, a Magician who can only work Charms. Spells and even Intermediate Magic are beyond their reach. The next Sector is a Spell Magician or Spellweaver. They are able to work Charms, Intermediate Magic, and Spells. The second highest Sector is an Enchanted. They are able to use basic to medium level Enchantments as well as the easier categories of Magic. The strongest Sector of Magicians is the CLAIMED, which was previously known as the High Enchanted until the True Master of Magic changed it when he* CLAIMED *everyone in that Sector for a specific purpose. The* CLAIMED *can work almost all Magic, but the most difficult Enchantments are too hard for the weaker of them.*

    Part Two: Magical Keys. A Magical Key is part of a Charm, usually the last word, which is absolutely necessary for the Charm to work. There are typically several versions of a Charm that will work. A variation of the Charm in Lesson One is:

If you want to see,
If you want to find me:
Spell the Spell and tell the Charm: Revealius!

In this Charm, Revealius *is the Key. Although you can perform a Charm with just the Key, it is much more difficult. The Key is—quite literally—the key to the Charm working.* The page ended.

    Well, Grace observed, *that was much shorter than yesterday's lesson. Not so much to absorb at once.* She studied the page until time for lunch, and afterwards she began her Magical applications time with the Master.

    Today Grace was able to survive about half an hour longer before she had to rest. The Master grinned at her, impressed. "You are growing stronger quickly, Grace. I am glad. Now, go rest." Once again, Grace obeyed, after taking the next lesson to her room along with her.

    This set the pattern for Grace's day—eat, study, eat, practice, sleep. Only on Sundays did they rest from studying, but instead they visited or talked among themselves. Grace was thankful for the day of rest and the time to get to know Andrea and Tom, who were becoming her first real friends.

And so the pattern formed in the little school in New Yorin.

6. The Master's Surprise

A month came and went. Grace became quite strong in Magic, so the Master promoted her to Tom and Andrea's class. Now the three of them studied together in the mornings, debating the less specific points in the lesson. In the afternoons, the Master gave them training in Spells from basic to intermediate levels.

Grace had learned a lot. She was proud of her achievements. Her skill had just barely surpassed Tom's, and she was improving every day. The Master declared that it would be a wonder if Grace did not grow even beyond the Master's own abilities, but her face twisted into a guarded expression as she proclaimed it. She appeared to have mixed emotions battling for control within her. There were pride and thankfulness, but Grace also detected a touch of fear in her eyes. What did the Master have to fear?

Occasionally Grace wondered how the others in the orphanage were doing. She had never been very close to any of them, but her many years spent there had formed a defensiveness for the other orphans in her heart. She wondered of any of them had been as fortunate as herself, but she doubted it. Nellie, of course would be continuing to prepare for college. Nellie was probably the most fortunate of the girls at the orphanage, but she was also the only one who was not an orphan.

Grace gave a forlorn sigh, but then she noticed the Master was speaking to her. "Grace. Grace!" Grace refocused on the scene around her.

It was lunchtime. Tom was teasing Andrea, and the Master had been talking to Grace about her studies when Grace had drifted off. "Grace." The Master frowned at her, not in reproof but in compassion. "What are you thinking of, child? You are not listening to me. What is on your mind?"

Grace blinked. "Nothing. I'm fine. Just tired, that's all. What were you saying?"

The Master narrowed her eyes, detecting Grace's lie. She decided to ignore it. "I had asked you if you succeeded in working just the Keys of those Charms."

"Well... kind of. Some of them worked, but some didn't."

"Which ones didn't?" queried the Master.

"The Specifius one and the Obsura Delicia one," Grace answered. "I tried them several times, but they just didn't work."

The Master smiled. "I think the first one didn't work because it is Spectifius, not Specifius. I'm not sure what's wrong with Obsura Delicia, though. We'll have to work on that sometime."

"Yes," agreed Grace.

"Not today, however. In fact, I believe that we will not work on that Charm for a while yet. I have special plans for this afternoon. If Tom will ever finish his lunch, that is. I must have *all* of you present, seeing as there aren't very many of you."

Tom grinned but stopped poking Andrea. "I'm not hungry for lunch. I want dessert," he whined.

"Not today. We have wasted much time eating anyway. If you really are not hungry, then we will move on to our...well, lesson, but not really."

The three CLAIMED looked at her with curiosity, but she would not reveal more. Quickly they stood, allowing the table to sit out uncleaned for once, and hurried to their chairs before the Master. She looked at them with a twinkle in her eye. "Today I want to share with you a secret and a surprise. First, the secret. Only a select few know about it."

The children looked at her expectantly. "Yes?"

The Master lifted something from out of the pillows on the chair and held it into the light. Tom looked at it and wrinkled his nose in disgust. "That's it? Just an old conch shell?"

"Just a shell, but not conch." The Master's gaze teased them. She said no more, but smiled at them, urging them to question her or to figure it out on their own.

Grace studied the shell. As Tom had observed, it appeared to be a normal, slightly dirty shell, nothing more. She understood why he had shown immediate disgust, even though she did not agree with him. "What is it?" she queried finally.

The Master beamed at her. "It is the Shell of Secrets, Enchanted by the True Master's youngest sister. If you were to tell it a secret, it would remember it and reveal it to the person you intended to hear it at the time you intended them to hear it. To no other person and at no other time would it reveal the secret."

"Cool," responded Andrea, eyebrows raised in appreciation.

"I see," answered Grace. "I wonder how many secrets have been told to it, and who received them."

The Master's eyes held a far off look, as though she was thinking of the answer and it pained her. After few seconds, she replied, "I don't know. Maybe thousands, maybe hundreds. Maybe more, maybe less. Who knows?"

"Why are you showing your shell to us?" asked Tom saucily.

Andrea glared at him, but the Master simply answered, "Most of the secrets in this shell have to do with the destiny of the CLAIMED. That is why the shell is here, in this School. I don't know for sure, but there could be secrets in here for you, even though it is not the right time for you to know them yet."

"But you won't tell us what the destiny is!" Tom protested.

"Be patient, Thomas. I will tell you when you are ready," the Master spoke to all of them, even though she looked solely at Tom. Then, in a louder voice, she announced, "And now, the surprise. Do you remember, Andrea and Tom, when I told you that there would be another CLAIMED joining the School?"

"Yes," they responded in unison. "Grace," Andrea completed.

"Correct. None of you know this yet, but there are more CLAIMED—four more. All of them live in the Normal Dimension."

"Oh!" exclaimed Grace. "Our class will more than double its size! When are they coming?"

"That is what I am about to explain," replied the Master. "You are not going to wait on them to come here this time. You three are going to get them."

The fact that entered Grace's mind was exclaimed by Andrea first. "But none of us have a license to travel between Dimensions!"

Tom snorted in derision. "We are going to another Dimension and *that* is what you think of? Really."

The Master ignored Tom's comment. "True, Andrea. I have a solution for that problem. I will expect each of you to have earned your licenses by the time you leave. Also—" she smiled in anticipation "—Jerra will be going with you."

All of the children grinned. "When are we leaving?" Grace questioned.

"We have much preparation to do. Thus, I do not believe you will leave for another few weeks. However, you—*all* of you" she stared pointedly at Tom "—will have to spend that time wisely if you are to be prepared to leave within a month." The children nodded rapidly in understanding. The Master continued, "Good! Now, here is Lesson One Hundred Forty-Three: Travelling between Dimensions and Lesson Fifty-One: Initiation of Magic. I will see you three at dinner."

The children nodded. Scurrying as quickly as a mouse, Tom disappeared into his room. Andrea started toward her room, beckoning for Grace to follow, and Grace strode after her.

Andrea had been teaching Grace a game using cards and dice. It was not Magical, but it had an element of fun in it that was unlike any other game Grace had ever played.

She failed to guess that the fun came not from the game itself but from enjoying it with a friend.

In the game, there were two dice and one deck of cards, minus the aces, the sevens, and all of the face cards. Each player was dealt five cards. The youngest player—in this instance Grace—went first. Grace rolled the dice. If the total number displayed by the pair of dice matched a number in Grace's hand, then she got to discard the card. She had three tries to roll the dice before the next player's turn. However, if one of the players rolls a seven, ten, eleven, or twelve, then they have to draw a card instead of discarding one. The first player to discard all of their cards wins.

Andrea did not get the game out today, though. Instead, both she and Grace jumped up on the big bed.

"Well," began Andrea. "Isn't it crazy? I've never been to another Dimension! And now we're going to get the four new CLAIMED? It's...ridiculous." Her tone sounded slightly dazed, as if she couldn't believe what she was saying and she was trying to convince herself it was true.

"I guess it's not as bizarre for me," replied Grace, "because I grew up in that other Dimension. It may not be what I'm used to anymore, but it used to be my home, so in a way it feels like I'm just going back to reality. That scares me, though, because my old reality is something I never want to go back to. Still, I'm glad we're going. It will be good to expand the School."

Andrea nodded in understanding. "Not long ago there were just two of us. Now there's three—soon to be seven! The rate at which the School is growing is really miraculous."

"Our morning debates will be quite lively." Grace smiled in anticipation.

Andrea grinned back. "It seems like it would be hard for them to get more lively than now, with Tom being ridiculously loud one minute and falling asleep the next."

Grace glanced down at the Lessons that she held in her hands. "Travelling between Dimensions—I know what that's about—but Initiation of Magic? I wonder…" She glanced at Andrea for an explanation.

Andrea nodded. "When Jerra came to get you, did she do something? —It probably felt like electricity."

"Yes," Grace answered, puzzled as to where Andrea was going with this.

"It made your eyes green, for one thing, but it also made it possible for you to use the Magical power stored in your mind. That was your Initiation. I guess the reason we're learning this is we will have to Initiate the Magic in the other CLAIMED."

"That makes sense," agreed Grace. She remembered the shock of the electricity rushing up through her into her head. "I wonder if the person who does it—Jerra, in my case—feels the spark, too?"

Andrea shook her head. "I don't know. My Initiation and Discovery were so long ago I can hardly remember them."

"Jerra knows. I bet the Master does, too. I wonder who else knows."

Andrea looked up from the paper in her hand, a curious expression on her face. "Grace, is Jerra a Spell Magician or an Enchanted? I'm sure she's not CLAIMED."

Grace shrugged. "I have no idea. I was so confused when I met her that I hardly picked up any information. I didn't know about Might Sectors then, anyway. I guess she's probably a Spell Magician, though. It just seems like it."

Andrea gave Grace an inquisitive glance, but Grace did not try to explain why she felt that way. Grace couldn't have explained it even if she had tried. It was simply intuition. Andrea did not inquire further. Instead, she asked, "Do you want to play Three Chances? We have plenty of time to think about this later."

Readily, Grace agreed. Andrea set up the game, and they began to play.

***

That evening at dinner, conversation turned once more to the coming of the new CLAIMED. The children felt excited and glad that the School was expanding.

"Are any of these new people boys?" questioned Tom. "It's hard enough to be the only boy out of three, but the only one out of seven!" Tom shook his head. "No way."

The Master turned to him. "Actually, Tom, two of the new students are boys. That way we will have half boys and half girls—or as close as we can get with an odd number of students, at least."

"Good," responded Tom gladly.

43

"How do you know so much about them? For that matter, how do you even know they exist? How could you know how many Magicians are in the other Dimension at all?" Grace queried.

"That is a topic we will discuss closer to the time that you leave. We have extensive studies for you to do before you go. I cannot thoroughly lecture you on a topic like that at the table, so we will wait until another time." The Master's tone indicated that she had formed a lesson plan long before the three inquisitive teenagers began asking questions, and that she intended to stick to that plan. She added, almost as an afterthought, but not quite, "Good question, though. It is an important principal."

Grace nodded.

Andrea asked, "Why do you want *us* to go get them? After all, shouldn't we be learning stuff instead of travelling?"

"You will be learning. This will be very valuable practice in how to work Magic. You cannot learn some of these concepts by simply reading, and they can't be practiced here. Thus, you must leave to learn this."

"I see."

The Master smiled at her. "I am glad. Now, you three should probably go to bed. Tomorrow will be a long day."

The children nodded and quickly got ready for bed. Before long, they were all asleep.

7. Training

Studying began in earnest the next morning. The three CLAIMED learned about the simple Spell of Initiation and the Intermediate Magic of travelling between Dimensions. The Master frowned, staring at the children. "This first technique is quite essential, but it poses a substantial problem, as well. You must be able to Initiate the new CLAIMED, but no one has ever found a way to practice this particular Spell. You must simply read the lesson to learn how the Magic works, and try to complete the Spell as best as you can when the time comes. If necessary, Jerra can complete the Spell for you." The Master smiled at Grace. "She's certainly had enough practice."

Travelling between the Dimensions was another matter altogether. First, the Master had them memorize the words. Because the Magic only worked if they controlled the Magic while speaking the words, the Master had the children recite the words out loud without Magic until they could remember them correctly and used perfect pronunciation. After that, she had them do other pieces of Intermediate Magic of similar difficulty. She would not let them try to transport themselves to another Dimension until after they received their licenses, but she promised she would take them to be tested in three days, on Friday. In the meantime, they would practice Intermediate Magic and learn the rules of when and where it was necessary to practice Magic in the Normal Dimension. It would certainly create an extremely difficult circumstance if they used it

45

while they were being observed by someone non-Magical. (The Master's rule for Magic in Normality was only to use it while Initiating Magic and travelling between the Dimensions, unless it would endanger their lives not to use it.)

On Friday, as promised, the Master took the children to be tested for their licenses. At the building (which was called Center for Magical Licenses, all kinds and quantities), the three CLAIMED were each led into a separate room for a written examination. On it they wrote their name, their age, and their Might Sector before they answered the questions on Magical Theory, Charms, Spells, Intermediate Magic, and Magical caution in other Dimensions. Grace excelled because she knew more about the other Dimension than the others, but they all passed the test.

After the written exam, the children verbally answered a series of questions on the Magic that they had learned so far. Finally, each of the children had to transport themselves and one Center for Magical Licenses employee to the corresponding building in New York. Then the young CLAIMED had to transport themselves and the employees back. All of the employees were impressed, thus all three of the children walked triumphantly back to School holding their own licenses. All three children fell asleep that night, full of relief and exhaustion.

The next week the children studied how to locate Magic in another Dimension. Tom found the topic thoroughly boring. In his mind, it did not matter how anyone knew that the other CLAIMED were there. He was just ready to be on the road. The Master, of course, ignored his view on the matter. He studied the material, so she had no reason to scold him.

The new topic enthralled Andrea and Grace. They discovered that it, too, was a form of Intermediate Magic; it was spoken but had to do with human beings. Whenever a person was Found, they heard the Finding Phrase in their head. Grace remembered the conversation she had had with the Master on her first night in the Magic Dimension. She wondered if the Master had thought any more on what the addition to Grace's Finding Phrase meant, but she decided not to mention it at the moment. Also, the children learned that Magic could only be used to search a certain amount of land at once. The Magic had to be repeated several times, even if the searcher knew the general location of the person they were trying to find. "Luckily for you," the Master announced, "Jerra has already located the four CLAIMED, so you don't have to search for them yourselves.

"If you were trying to find someone using this piece of Magic, you would have to be looking at a map of the area where you are searching. The location of the person would then start to glow on the map."

"But how do you know there aren't any more CLAIMED in the other Dimension?" asked Grace curiously.

"Because travel between Dimensions is very strictly regulated," answered the Master. "Think about it this way: If you have to own a license or else you have to be travelling with someone who does for you to cross Dimensions, and if they have to inform someone in the Travel Regulation Building every time they leave or come back, then the building would know exactly how many people are in Normality, right? And licenses are fewer than you think."

"Okay, I get that. But what if someone, like my mother, has a baby in the other Dimension? Did the Building know I existed, and I that I was in the other Dimension?"

"The Building knew," answered the Master shortly, as though she was tired. She gave no further explanation.

"How many Magicians are in Normality right now?" questioned Tom.

"Eight, including the four CLAIMED. As you can see, there are very few," responded the Master. "When you three go with Jerra, there will still be only twelve in the whole Dimension."

"Well, how do you know those four are CLAIMED?" Grace persisted.

"The signal is stronger. The Finding signal, the one that glows on the map. It glows more brightly, even more so than if they were Enchanted," answered the Master.

Grace grinned. "Oh, I see. Finding is quite complicated, though."

"Yes, it is," the Master agreed. "It took thirteen years for us to Find you, because your parents gave us no hint to where you might be in the other Dimension. We knew you were there, we just didn't know where."

"Hey, that rhymes!" cried Andrea, looking up from the note she was rapidly scribbling down.

"Yes, it does." The Master glanced at Tom, who was staring out the window, his eyes unfocused. "Tom!"

His head shot up. "Yes! Yes?" he asked, looking around.

The Master shook her head. "Alright, children, that is enough for today. We will continue on with this lesson tomorrow. You are free to go. And Tom—" she studied him, her eyes dancing "—if you don't understand what we are talking about, please ask."

Tom flushed, embarrassed. "Yes, I will."

The girls quickly gathered up their lessons. As had become their routine, Grace dropped her notes in her room before heading to Andrea's to play Three Chances. Grace wondered what the Master did during this time. Once she asked Andrea about it.

"I have no idea," Andrea had responded. "She's always gone to her room after lessons, before dinner. It's her routine. She has never explained to us what she does in there, though. I believe it has something to do with locating the other CLAIMED, but that's just a guess. It could be anything."

Grace had her own guesses, too, and they weren't similar to Andrea's. At that moment, though, she chose to keep them to herself.

Grace blinked back to reality as Andrea announced, "It's your turn, Grace." Grace took the dice, avoiding eye contact with the others. She had three cards in her hand: a five, a two, and a nine. She rolled a three—then a nine. With a smile, she discarded. Then she rolled a seven. *Ugh,* she thought, as she drew a three. *That didn't help.*

Tom won that round. Andrea and Grace played for second place, and Andrea won. Grace laid down her hand—

a five and a three. Andrea shrugged. "It's okay. Do you want to play again?"

"Yes," Grace answered, so they played the time away until dinner.

***

At the beginning of the next week—the third week—the Master made an announcement. "This week we will be studying a topic that none of you have even hinted at studying before. Why now? Because in a week—next Monday—you will be leaving." The uproar was instantaneous and tremendous, despite the fact that it consisted of only three teenagers. The Master waited for them to calm down a little before she continued. "We will be studying parallelism in evil."

None of the young CLAIMED knew what she was talking about because this topic was only mentioned to those who would be travelling between Dimensions. "This week we will cover the topics of evil in Normality and evil in Magic as well as the similarity of structure and location of parallel Magic. We will also cover the topic of fighting evil in each of the Dimensions." The Master paused thoughtfully before continuing. "You may go for today. I will see you in the morning for lessons, because there is not a written lesson on this topic."

The children nodded and scrambled to collect their things. Andrea motioned for Grace to follow her, but Grace shook her head. "No, I have something I need to talk to the Master about. I wonder…" She paused. "Never mind. I'll see you at dinner." Grace had to talk to the Master before they left for the other Dimension, and Grace was not a person who liked to leave things until the last minute.

Andrea nodded without question. "Alright. See you at dinner, then." With a wave, she bounced off to her room. Grace knew Andrea was disappointed that she wasn't telling her everything, but Andrea had accepted that Grace had secrets, too.

Tom ran off to his room without a backward glance. Grace wondered what it was like in there. Tom obviously kept himself occupied with something, but Grace doubted he had video games like the boys in Normality. Slightly dazed, Grace shook her head as she realized that she was alone in the room with the Master. She turned to her teacher, whose eyes were questioning.

"You wanted to speak to me, Grace?" the Master asked gently.

"Oh, yes. Um—the first night I was here you were puzzled by the phrase '2nd to T.M.' Have you figured it out?"

The Master sighed. "Come into my room, Grace." Grace followed her, and the Master gestured for her to sit down. Grace obliged. "Well, Grace." The Master looked down at her hands. "The truth is—I lied to you."

"Huh?" Grace blinked, confused.

The Master looked at her, her eyes troubled. "I knew what it meant, even then." The Master sighed and studied Grace. Grace looked back, bewildered. She had never witnessed the Master like this before. The Master took a deep breath as though she was trying not to cry. "Look,

51

Grace. You don't understand all of this yet. You *can't* understand all of this yet. I will tell you the rest when the time is right, and when you are ready."

Grace nodded, her eyes wide.

"Alright," said the Master, trying to keep her voice steady. She looked down. "This is—hard. It is hard for me because I love you three like you are my own children. It will be hard for you later…" she trailed off, her eyes distant. After a few seconds she blinked and looked up. "I'm sorry. Never mind that now. This part is of the puzzle is actually quite interesting. It is just when you see how it fits in with the other pieces that things get scary."

Grace studied the Master. The Master looked back, her eyes asking Grace if Grace still wanted to know what was going on. "Tell me," Grace responded. "I need to know."

"Alright. Do you remember the first night you were here? I told you about Dimensions and the CLAIMED." The Master's voice did not waver. It was as though she had never looked frightened.

"I remember," Grace replied. "How could I forget?"

The Master smiled a little, although it did not reach her eyes. "And you remember the part in your lessons about how the True Master of Magic made the High Enchanted into the CLAIMED?"

"Yes," Grace confirmed.

"True Master. T.M. Have you not guessed what it stands for?" the Master questioned with raised eyebrows.

"I hadn't. Oh!" cried Grace.

The Master nodded. "And you remember that the True Master was the most powerful Magician ever… second to the True Master…" the Master extended her arm, inviting Grace to complete the sentence.

Grace's eyes had stretched as wide as saucers. "2nd to T.M. I'm the second most powerful Magician—ever?"

The Master nodded. "That is the answer to your query."

"That's ridiculous!" Grace exclaimed. "You're more powerful than me—and Jerra—and Andrea! I'm not—"

The Master held up her hand to stop her. "Nay. I simply have more practice. You have more *potential*; all you need is *practice*. I encourage you not to dwell on this discovery, though. You should probably not mention it to the twins yet, either. I do not want you to be a Magician full of power but full of vanity." Grace nodded. The Master continued, "You should probably rest before dinner. You have had a long day."

Grace nodded again, overcome with disbelief. She went to her room and lay on her bed, staring up at the ceiling. *2nd to T.M! Ridiculous! Absurd!* Eventually, she fell asleep.

The next day, the Master taught the children on the subject of evil in Normality. "Grace," she commanded, "Please tell us some of the forms of evil in Normality."

Grace began to explain. "In Normality there is a lot of fighting all around the world, especially in the Middle East. People get mad at one another and hurt—or kill—others for little things. And there are organized armies that fight one another so that their country will become more powerful. It is really awful." Grace shuddered.

The Master nodded grimly. "In this Dimension the Middle East is referred to as Mideos Eiste, in the continent of Asiana."

"Asia," Grace whispered, almost inaudibly. "It's Asia."

"Correct. Here, Asiana is a continent filled with terror, dread, fear, and hatred. Like the Middle East, Mideos Eiste is a place full of pain. Do you know why I tell you this?"

"So we can have good geography?" Tom asked, with one eyebrow raised.

"No," responded the Master. "Not that. Try again— Andrea?"

Andrea nodded. "So that we don't go to a place in Normality where there is evil in Magic? Because there will be evil there in Normality, too," she guessed.

"Good!" exclaimed the Master. "The same quantity of evil, having the same effect, but in different form. In this Dimension we have Magical evils, and in Normality they have evil that is just as dreadful in things such as the misuse of firearms, bombs, missiles, and other things besides. These things are just as dreadful; they just come in a different *form*. This said, do you understand why you must not go somewhere in Normality where there is evil in Magic?"

The children nodded rapidly.

"Good," the Master finished.

Wednesday was the next day. The Master addressed them as usual. "Yesterday we talked about evil in Normality. Today I want to tell you about evil in Magic. As you know, a great deal of evil exists in Mideos Eiste, although it is gathering force and moving out into the rest of Asiana. This evil exists in the form of what we call the Darkniss. The Darkniss is a being of incredible evil and power. Where smoke, explosions, and terror reign in the Middle East, in Mideos Eiste there is the dark fog. It is a cold, sinister fog, with little moisture, and when you are inside it you feel like you are suffocating. In this fog dwell the Darkniss' minions, creatures known as the Eldritch. The Eldritch are creatures who have let pieces of the Darkniss inside of them, causing them to become shriveled and gray. Despite their shrunken appearance, do not underestimate them. They are very strong, and those who were Magical before they became Eldritch now control Dark Magic. I hope you never meet them, but you never know. Alright, that is good for today. I don't want to creep you out completely, but I thought you should be warned, should you ever have to deal with a creature that looked like a powerful gray raisin." She smiled without humor. "Now, you may go."

Grace stood wearily. The Master laid a kind hand on her shoulder. "Do not be troubled, child. It is a wonderful talent that you have."

Grace shook her head. The others had left the room, and she sighed audibly. "It's not fair! Andrea works so hard, and has for so long, and yet I surpass her in only a few months. It's—wrong! I don't want to have more Magic than my friends!"

"Everyone has different levels of power within their Might Sector. It is not unusual to be stronger—or weaker—than your closest friends. You may be more powerful, and you may not *have* to work as hard, but you should work just as devotedly. You don't want to belittle your skill. You need to work just as hard as Andrea, if not more. It is totally fair. Now, do not think about this too much. I advise you to go do something with your friends—you need to relax before Monday comes, okay?"

Grace nodded. "Alright. See you tomorrow, then."

The Master smiled. "Not at dinner tonight?" she asked teasingly.

Grace finally smiled with her. "Yes, you're right. See you tonight." The Master nodded at her, and Grace left the hall.

Thursday dawned. The Master did not lecture them today, but instead she handed them several sheets of paper.

"What's this?" Andrea questioned.

"A test," Tom observed.

He was right. Reluctantly, Grace studied her parchment for a minute before asking, "Is this a test on all we have learned the past few weeks?"

"Yes." The Master nodded. "Today, you will have this written examination, and tomorrow, I will test you physically in your Magical skill. Saturday, you will get ready to leave, and Sunday—"

"We'll play and rest," interrupted Tom.

"Well, yes, that too, but Jerra is coming on Sunday. She will tell you her plan for the trip and give you some tips—she has a lot of experience, so you all need to listen." She looked pointedly at Tom, who looked back innocently. "I will leave now so you can finish your tests. Once they are complete, leave them outside my door. I will give them back to you in the morning." She left.

Grace began to read the test.

1. What type of Magic do both Finding and Dimension-travelling fall under?

2. What is the Key for Dimension-travelling?

3. What is the Key for Finding?

4. What are the words used for Dimension-travelling?

5. What are the words used for Finding?

6. Describe Dimension-travelling, the process of getting a license, and how the Travel Regulation Building knows how many people are in Normality.

7. What is a Finding Phrase?

8. How much land does a single Finding cover?

9. What piece of paper is critical to have in front of you while performing a Finding?

10. How do you Find someone and pinpoint their location?

11. How many Magicians are in Normality right now?

12. How do you know which Might Sector a person is in if you have successfully Found them?

13. Describe parallelism in evil.

14. Why can you not go somewhere in Normality where there is evil in the Magic Dimension?

15. What is the parallel of Asia?

16. What is the parallel of the Middle East?

17. Describe the Darkniss.

18. Describe Dark fog.

19. Describe the Eldritch and their connection to Dark Magic.

20. Where is the majority of the Darkniss located?

Grace thought, *Well, that's thorough.* Slowly, though, she began to fill in the answers, as did Andrea and Tom.

When she had answered the last question, she glanced at the Magical clock above the doorway. *Oh my!* she exclaimed mentally. *It's four-thirty!* She shoved her pen away across the table, folded her work neatly, and strode to the Master's door, where she left her papers. Andrea had long since completed her work, and Tom was just finishing up, but Grace decided to go to her room instead of going to play Three Chances with the others.

The Master had given her a few books to occupy the shelves in Grace's closet. Grace now selected the old, stained book titled simply *The History.* Grace flipped it open to a random page, thankful that the history of the Magic Dimension was so interesting.

On a bright day in the year 2001, the Gemini Buildings stood tall. In a few hours they would be burned to the ground because a dragon commanded by a cruel rider would fly into them, dousing them in flames. This disaster became known as the disaster of September 11. Grace

58

realized, *That's parallel to 9-11 with the Twin Towers. It's—it's exactly the same!*

Grace rushed into the hall when she heard the clock chime six times. After taking her place opposite Andrea, beside the Master, they all spoke the Charm for dinner and began to eat. When dinner was finished and Andrea and Tom had already left, the Master gave Grace a small smile. "See you tomorrow, child."

Grace nodded and watched the Master leave the room. With a sigh, she entered her room and began to ready herself for bed.

On Friday night the Master treated the children to the Magical version of a movie. It was a complicated Charm, now worked by the Master, displaying in the air an Illusion of a different place and different people. The people moved and spoke in the room, acting out the story. When the movie was over, the Master breathed a sigh of relief while the children gave her a standing ovation. She gave a little bow, and the children headed to their separate rooms. They were tired, and tomorrow would be a busy day. Tomorrow they would be getting ready to leave for another Dimension!

8. Departure

Grace awoke with a jolt, the memory of her dream coursing through her. She had been young in the dream, but she didn't know how young. She could hear bears growling as they tore through her house. She could hear the screams of her mother and older brother as well as the frantic shouting of her father. She could smell the metallic scent of blood as she huddled deeper into the covers of her bed. Eventually, the moaning stopped, and the house fell silent. Too silent. Her parents were dead.

Grace gave a little gasp. Sweat beaded her forehead, running in streams down into her eyes. She blinked frantically. She wondered if the dream had really happened. It had been so vivid. If it *had* really happened, why had she just dreamt it? She heard the clock chime twice. It was still the middle of the night. With a sigh, Grace dried her face on the sheets before rolling over and eventually falling back to sleep.

When Grace awoke again, it was long past breakfast time. Andrea and Tom were each in their respective rooms, probably packing for their upcoming journey. Grace's belly gave a ferocious growl, so Grace crossed the hall and knocked on the Master's door.

"Yes?" the Master poked her head out. "Oh, good, you're awake. How was your sleep last night?"

Grace shuddered. "Not very good. I had a—bad dream."

The Master nodded. "I am sorry about that. Are you hungry? There are a few biscuits in the room to the right of yours. After you eat, you should pack. You will find a sack next to your breakfast."

Grace nodded. "Thanks."

As always, the food was splendid. Grace always wondered at the fact that it was still warm, but the question never crossed her mind when she was with the Master. Grace allowed the biscuit to crumble in her mouth, filling it with buttery goodness.

The biscuit was gone all too soon, so Grace grabbed the sack and headed to her room. *Only get essentials,* she thought. A grin lit her face and she began to hum "Bare Necessities" as she worked. Soon she had all her clothes and her hair brush neatly in the sack. The Master had recommended that they just pack these and buy the rest of the necessities when they entered Normality. The Master did pack each of them a dinner package. "Save these and use them when you need a treat. I dare say that you will want them before you return."

Grace, Andrea, and Tom left their sacks in a pile on top of their shoes, next to the door that went outside. The Master let them do what they wanted with the rest of the day, so Grace taught the twins how to play some of the games from Normality such as hide-and-seek, tag, and Slap Jack. Tired, sweaty, and out of breath, they fell on to the plush couch in the game room.

"This is so fun. When the others get here, then imagine! It will be epic!" Tom threw his arms wide.

Grace laughed. "They just have to get here, that's all."

The grin melted off Andrea's face. "We're leaving in two days. I wonder how long we'll be gone. I'm just glad that Jerra's coming, too. She's had a lot of experience doing this sort of stuff."

Grace nodded. "I wonder how she got involved in this? It's not like she's CLAIMED, or anything."

Tom shrugged. "I guess she just likes us?"

Andrea rolled her eyes at her twin brother. She responded sarcastically, "Absolutely. She dedicated her life to finding CLAIMED because she likes *us?* Think about it, Tom; that makes no sense at all."

Tom crossed his arms. "Fine. Think that. 'It makes no sense at all...'" He snorted. "It's just a theory, okay? No need to get all mad."

"Look who's talking," scoffed Andrea.

"Cut it out, guys," Grace finally interfered. "We can ask Jerra herself. She'll be here tomorrow."

Andrea and Tom both nodded, but Tom shot Andrea a venomous glare. Grace sighed. Frequent arguments were a downside to having twins as her best friends and only schoolmates. *Not for long,* she reminded herself. *No, don't think so much about leaving. You can worry about that tomorrow.* She followed her friends into the hall for another game of Tag.

Sunday morning dawned, as bright and as beautiful as a spring Sunday ought to be. The Master hurried around with the children on her heels, tidying up with a snap of her well-trained fingers, and preparing a room for Jerra, who would arrive that afternoon. The excitement was infectious. The Master whistled as she worked, while the children chatted and giggled. All four of them were trying not to think about the next morning; the Master because she loved the three teenagers like they were her own children, and the children because they did not know what the adventure would hold.

Jerra arrived just after lunch. She was greeted calmly by the Master but with exclamations from the children. After leaving her things in the room next to Andrea's, she allowed the children to pull her around, laughing as if she were a child, too. She happily joined in hide-and-seek, which she already knew how to play from years of work in Normality. Being only twenty-six, she felt that it was not a horrible thing to play like she was a child again.

That evening, the children and the Master followed Jerra into her room to talk. All five of them squeezed on to the bed. The Master began, "Okay, Jerra. Tomorrow you and the children are leaving. Can you give us your plans for your trip into Normality?"

Jerra nodded. "As all of you know, the purpose of this trip is to collect the four CLAIMED in Normality." She fished inside the pocket of her coat for four little scrolls. She handed one to each member of the group and they unrolled the pieces of parchment. Each map depicted the United States of America, with four little stars on it. Beside each star sat a small number. "These maps," Jerra continued, "show the locations of the said four CLAIMED. You may also have noticed that four of us are going on this trip. Here is the plan: We will travel together to get the first CLAIMED, and I will bring him back here. The thing is—I will not be coming back. After I have left, you three will travel to get the second CLAIMED. Tom, you will be responsible for bringing her back here. You will not travel back, but instead you will stay here so that the new CLAIMED will have someone more experienced to help them. Girls, you will travel on to get the third CLAIMED. It will be Andrea's turn to bring him safely back here. This, of course, leaves Grace. You will travel by yourself to get the last CLAIMED and bring her back to the School. By then we will all have returned."

The Master nodded. "It is a good plan. I am glad they will have you to lead them, Jerra." She gave Jerra a warm smile. "It will be lonely around here for a little while, but soon I will have new students to mentor!" She looked around thoughtfully for a moment before continuing, "Go rest now, children. It is late, and tomorrow will be a long day." She glanced at Jerra. "I am sure you want to get an early start in the morning, but it would be best if the children slept in. They will need their rest."

"Of course," Jerra replied, smiling. "I will need the sleep, too."

"That's settled, then." The Master clapped her hands. "Off to bed, you three! Good night."

"Good night," the children chorused, clambering off the bed and heading to their own rooms.

The Master smiled a tired smile. "Good night, Jerra. I will see you tomorrow."

"Yes. See you," Jerra responded. The Master left the room, and they all headed to bed.

64

***

Grace dreamed once again of her house being destroyed by a bunch of wolves. When she woke up, panting, she realized that the dream had continued longer tonight.

In her dream, she had crept out of bed. She had not entered her parents' or older brother's rooms, but instead tiptoed to the front of the house. She had heard voices of men and women talking outside of the walls. She heard one say, "The Enchantment has taken hold of her instead." *What Enchantment?* she wondered. *Instead of what?* Then Grace had awoken.

Unsettled, Grace crept out into the main hall. She could barely glimpse the light shining out from under the Master's door, but it was there. She walked over the door, and it opened itself. The Master, who had been working at the desk, looked up. "Hello, Grace. Can't sleep?"

Grace shook her head. "More nightmares."

The Master raised her eyebrows. "Come in. You can rest in here if you want. I have had my share of dreams, too." She suddenly appeared very weary.

Grace stepped inside. "Thanks."

The Master nodded in acknowledgement. "You should try to sleep. You will need to rest before tomorrow."

"Okay," Grace responded, her voice dull and tired. She tried to sleep, but the light was too bright. Finally she decided to head back to her room and brave the nightmares. After tossing around for a while, she got comfortable and

65

fell back to sleep. She was glad that dreams were gone for the night.

Monday morning dawned. The day felt dreary. As soon as Grace saw the foreboding clouds outside of the window, she wished all the more that they were going to stay safe and sound at the School, instead of heading off into another Dimension. Most of all, she wished that Jerra would stay with them the whole trip, instead of leaving them alone to complete the task.

But that was impossible. They were, after all, CLAIMED; Jerra was not responsible for them. This was *their* path, not Jerra's, and they were going to follow it. Grace sighed. Nonetheless, the morning did not feel radiant, and Grace wished they were just staying at the School.

She turned to the room where she would eat her breakfast, since she had missed breakfast because she had slept in. As usual, she found the steaming biscuits waiting on her.

After breakfast, Grace paced into the hall, where she found the Master and Jerra speaking in low voices next to the door. She hesitated, wondering where Andrea and Tom were, but not wanting to interrupt by asking. The Master solved her dilemma by turning away from Jerra. "Good morning, Grace. If you want to find your friends, they are in the game room." She pointed to the door. "However, I suggest that you get dressed first."

"Thanks," Grace responded, taking the Master's advice and heading back to her room.

When she emerged half an hour later, she was neatly dressed, with her hair slicked back in a tight braid. She hurried to join her friends in their game of Three Chances. None of them spoke; they were all too busy thinking about their rapidly approaching journey. Even Tom was silent, his uncharacteristically solemn face bent over his hand of cards.

Soon, Jerra entered the room. All three teenagers looked up expectantly. "Good morning," she greeted the children. "We are leaving in an hour. Thought you might want to know." She glanced around at their faces. "You're quite gloomy this morning," she observed. "Come on! We're going to another Dimension. It'll be fun, okay?"

The children nodded, reluctant to admit that they would be homesick. Jerra accepted this, remembering that she had once felt the same way. "Well," she continued, "are you going to invite me to sit down, or should I invite myself?" Andrea smiled and patted the spot beside her.

In an hour, the four got up silently. They strode to the front door, where they picked up their packs and put on their shoes. The Master gave each of them, including Jerra, a tight hug and whispered, "I'll miss you." The twins, who had known her longer, couldn't speak without crying, so they merely nodded. Grace was able to whisper back, "You, too." Jerra didn't respond at all.

The door opened for them, and they emerged into the outside world.

9. Jerra's Story

Jerra stood still for a moment before beckoning to the children and beginning to walk toward the alleyway where Grace had first arrived in the Magic Dimension. "This is where we typically do the Dimension-travelling Magic, because people in the Normal Dimension rarely come here," explained Jerra. She seized Andrea's and Tom's hands, and Grace grasped Andrea's. The children heard Jerra whisper, and with a jolt, the world popped out of existence. In a few seconds, it reappeared, jarring the group as if on impact. Now, though, they could hear the honking of cars and the chatter of people. They were no longer in New Yorin, but now in New York.

"Woah," Andrea gasped in awe. "Is it always so loud here?"

Grace nodded. "Pretty much. Even at night."

Jerra pulled them on to the sidewalk, although they were forcefully jostled by the crowd. Jerra had to shout for the children to hear her. "Follow me," she commanded. The words she voiced were simple, but she had a hard time getting the children to understand her meaning.

The group trudged through the mass of people for what seemed like hours before Grace gave a shout and pointed. "The orphanage!" she cried, stopping in her tracks.

Jerra turned. "I know, Grace. But we need to keep going, okay?" Grace followed as they continued to move, but she wondered what it would be like in there if she went in. They wouldn't remember her, of that she felt sure. *Not even Nellie,* she thought sadly. *Of course, Nellie's probably off somewhere getting ready for college.* Suddenly, a query popped into her head. *I wonder if there are Magical colleges?*

When she asked, Jerra answered, "Yes, we do. Few and scattered, but they do exist. I never got to go, but many in our Dimension are blessed enough to graduate from college."

Maybe I will get to go to college, after all, Grace rejoiced mentally.

After a while, Jerra stopped in front of a house. The group had recently left the big city, and the children were wondering if they would get to rest at all on this journey. Apparently the answer was yes. Jerra knocked, and the three children huddled in a small group behind her.

The door opened. A tall, middle-aged woman with graying hair poked her head out. "Oh, it's you, Jerra!" she exclaimed, the relief obvious in her tone. "Come in, come in. I haven't seen you in a few months, so I thought a visit was due. To tell you the truth, I was beginning to worry."

"Hello, Gretchen," Jerra responded. "You shouldn't worry. But it *has* been a long time, so I honestly can't blame you."

"Em-hmm…" murmured Gretchen. "How is the curse holding up?"

"Hush!" cried Jerra, gesturing to the children.

"Oh!" Gretchen noticed the three teenagers for the first time. "Hello, kids. Come in, all of you. I have a few bedrooms upstairs that you may spend the night in—where are you currently headed?"

"Hartford, Connecticut," answered Jerra shortly, as the four travelers entered Gretchen's home.

"Good, good. Here is some good, hot soup—no Magical packets needed here!—and some bread and butter. Make yourselves at home."

"Thanks, Gretchen," Jerra replied with a smile, obviously relaxing now that the door to the outside world had been closed. "I really don't know what I'd do without you."

"No thanks needed, although I appreciate it. You are the reason I'm here in this Dimension in the first place," Gretchen smiled.

The children ate gladly. Tom consumed the most, but all of them ate their fair share and more.

When the group finished eating, Gretchen led them upstairs. She took Jerra to the room where she usually stayed, and she took Tom to another room down the hall. She led the girls to the third and last room. "I'm sorry," she apologized, "but we have limited space, so you two will have to share."

Andrea grinned. "We don't mind. It'll be like having a sleepover. I haven't had a sleepover since I was seven."

Grace nodded. "This is great, Ms.... I'm sorry, I don't know your last name."

"Gretchen. Just call me Gretchen."

"Okay. Well, thank you, Ms. Gretchen," continued Grace. "Thank you. It's just wonderful."

"Alright, girls," replied Gretchen with a smile. "I'll be downstairs if you need anything. See you tomorrow."

"Okay," the girls responded as Gretchen left the room.

Andrea and Grace collapsed into their beds, exhausted. They forgot to even turn off the lights. Or, rather, Grace forgot to turn out the lights; Andrea did not understand light switches yet.

✳ ✳ ✳

Grace bit her lip, frustrated. She tasted blood, and she could feel tears dripping down her face. *Why?* she wondered. *Why am I constantly plagued by this dream? It makes no sense!* She gasped, clambering out of bed. She glanced at Andrea, hoping that she had not awoken her friend.

At the door, she flipped the light off. She found it difficult to resist slamming the door, but she resisted the temptation anyway. *What is wrong with me?* she screamed mentally. *What is WRONG with me?!?*

Grace stumbled down the hall to Jerra's room. *I just need to talk to someone,* she reasoned. *Maybe if I talk to someone it will go away.*

Jerra was already awake. It was only five-thirty in the morning, so she was surprised when her door flew open and hit the wall, followed by a thirteen-year-old girl who had tears streaming down her face. Jerra stood up abruptly. "Grace?" she asked, rapidly taking in the situation. "Come. Sit on my bed." Nodding, Grace obeyed. Jerra closed the door quietly. "What's wrong, child?"

Grace drew a deep breath, trying to calm herself. "I'm such a baby! But I'm so frustrated, and it won't stop!"

Jerra raised her eyebrows in confusion. "Whoa. Slow down. What won't stop?"

"This nightmare," sobbed Grace. "This is the third time! And it won't go away, it just keeps coming back! Why won't it go away, Jerra?" Her voice wavered and broke off.

"What nightmare?" Jerra persisted.

"It goes like this: I'm in this house in the woods. When I wake up, there are wolves in the house. The wolves—they kill my parents and my older brother. I feel like my family is really being murdered. It's—dreadful." Grace shuddered.

Jerra's face betrayed her obvious shock. "You dreamt that?" she whispered.

"Yes," Grace continued to sob. "Isn't it awful?" Grace looked up at Jerra. Her eyes widened and she jumped towards her friend.

Jerra had gone as white as a sheet, but she shook Grace off. "I'm fine," she stated, although her voice came out in a whimper. She began to pace. Grace sat back down on the bed, uneasy. Suddenly Jerra turned to Grace, her eyes haunted. "Can I tell you something?"

Grace nodded, her eyes wide. She had stopped crying in her fright over Jerra's reaction.

"That happened. Your dream really did happen." Jerra glanced at the younger girl. Her eyes were bloodshot. It looked as though she was trying not to cry.

"I had and older brother?" queried Grace, not understanding.

"No. It didn't happen to you. It happened to me."

"What?" Grace made a confused face.

"When I was seven, my house was attacked by bears. They killed my family, but not me. Our neighbors heard the commotion, but they were too late. They took me home with them."

"In my dream the neighbors said that the Enchantment had taken hold of you instead. What Enchantment? Instead of what?"

"Instead of my sister," answered Jerra sullenly.

Grace blinked. "But in my dream you didn't have a sister! What Enchantment, though?"

Jerra began to pace again. "Yes, I did have a sister. When I was born, I had a twin. An identical twin. She was CLAIMED, but she died when she was two because she was very sick. You ask what Enchantment?" Jerra snorted. "There are too many Enchantments surrounding the CLAIMED, in my opinion. I don't suppose you've ever heard of the curse of the CLAIMED?"

"No," Grace responded, following Jerra's pacing with her eyes.

"Have you ever thought about the fact that all CLAIMED are orphans? Every last one. Even the Master. I am sure you know they can't get married, either. Why, though?" Jerra paused. "No, don't answer. There are more Enchantments surrounding the CLAIMED than you can count. Well, not all Enchantments are without flaws. Emily may have escaped the curse, but then it fell on me instead, even though I am not CLAIMED. Me, an orphan. Have you ever wondered why I do this work? Because I have to. The curse makes sure I'm doing something helpful to the destiny. I don't have a choice."

Grace was taken aback by Jerra's outburst. "Oh, Jerra."

Jerra stopped pacing and sat on the bed beside Grace. "I am sorry to burden you with my bitter ramblings. I just find it—hard—to carry out someone else's work, especially considering I did not have a choice in the matter. But at least I'm doing something worthwhile. And I *do* enjoy travelling. But I wish that I had a choice."

Grace looked up, her expression thoughtful. "Why did I have your dream?"

Jerra frowned. "It's not unusual, actually. I Initiated your Magic, so you know things about me that not everyone does. It's a normal side effect of Initiation. But..." Jerra sighed. "It did bring back unwanted memories."

Grace nodded silently. Jerra looked up at the clock. "Well, it's six o' clock. If you want to get any more sleep, I would advise that you go back to bed." And just like that, as if she had not just told Grace some of the most deeply buried secrets of her past, she smiled and dismissed Grace from the room.

"Oh, and if you have any other strange, persistent dreams, come talk to me. They are probably about me, after all." Jerra smiled grimly.

Grace nodded. "Thanks, Jerra. And—I'm sorry. I had no idea."

Jerra merely sighed. "Good night, Grace."

"Good night, Jerra." Back in her bed, Grace wondered at what Jerra had told her. She remembered

Jerra's words of several months ago. *"You will never be able to go back to your place in that orphanage, no matter how scared or frustrated you get."* Grace grimaced. *How right you were, Jerra,* she mused.

10. The Argument

It's Tuesday! was Grace's first thought when her eyes flew open at eight-thirty in the morning. *A new day, a second day!* She whistled as she made up the bed, waking Andrea in the process.

Andrea blinked. Typically, she rose earlier than this, but the long stretch of walking yesterday had reduced her to a rare state of exhaustion. She looked confused for a moment before her eyes focused and she, too, jumped out of bed. "Good morning!" she cried. She spun around and fell back on the bed, laughing. "I'm in another Dimension, far from all I've ever known, and it's so good to be here. Think, yesterday we were all sad, but now we're excited and happy. It's so mixed up and wonderful!"

Grace laughed at her friend's enthusiasm. She threw a pillow at Andrea before turning back to the half-made bed.

The breakfast table was quiet that morning. After they finished eating, they went back upstairs to gather their things. The four travelers left Gretchen's house around mid-morning.

That was a long day. Gretchen had let Jerra take the car, so the four were not walking, but there was nothing to do on the way. Hour after hour, the children stared out the window at the terrain flashing past. They hardly spoke at all.

At noon, they went through a drive-through. This was a new experience for Andrea and Tom. They were fascinated by the way Jerra could just speak, and someone's voice would repeat the order, even though no one was standing by the car. ("It's way stranger than Magic. It's crazy!" Tom had remarked. Grace had responded, "It's technology.")

In the evening, the four pulled into a hotel in Waterbury, Connecticut. The doors confused the twins. Most of the doors that they had encountered in Normality had to be opened manually, but the doors at the front of the hotel opened on their own. Andrea mentioned this to Grace, and Grace chuckled. "Technology," she repeated.

The hotel room contained two large beds and a couch. Tom took the couch. He stuck out his tongue at the girls. "You two have to share," he taunted. He—of course—was right. Grace and Andrea took one bed and Jerra took the other. The four collapsed into sleep.

The next morning, Andrea and Tom were once more confounded by modern technology at the continental breakfast. The waffle maker especially fascinated them. Tom had frowned. "The waffle is super goopy, and then you wait, and then it becomes an actual *waffle*," he had remarked. After breakfast, they all got back on the road.

It was early afternoon when the small car drove in to Hartford. Jerra pulled into a driveway in front of what appeared to be an empty house. Why was she coming here?

"Get out, kids," she commanded, smiling at them. She strode up to the front door before pulling an enormous keyring out of her pocket. She bit her lip as she began twisting the keys around the ring. She searched in vain for the right key among about seventy keys. The children scrambled out of the car. "Could you please lock the car?" Jerra spoke firmly without looking up. Grace obeyed without question. It took about five minutes, but Jerra finally gave a cry of victory as she unlocked the building.

The children followed Jerra inside. For a house that from the outside appeared as if it had not been inhabited in several years it was in pristine condition. The floor sparkled as though it had been recently scrubbed and the furniture was well-dusted, but what surprised Grace the most was that when she reached to open a door, it opened itself for her. Jerra laughed at Grace's astonished face.

"Magic?" Grace frowned. "Here?"

Jerra grinned at her. "Magic," she repeated. "Here."

"How?" Grace questioned simply.

"This house belongs to a Magician. The Magician who lives in the corresponding house in the Magic Dimension owns it for the sole purpose of letting travelling Magicians—like us—have a place to stay. You might be surprised to know how many places like this there are scattered all over the country."

"I doubt I would be shocked," Grace responded, grinning. "Your keyring is evidence enough."

Jerra smiled back. "Be that as it may, I do not have keys to even two percent of the houses like this in America. Still, my collection has developed over the years. I had to start labeling them just to keep them straight. It still takes me a while to find the correct key. I guess I'll figure out a system eventually, though."

Grace nodded. "I'm sure you will." Her face was glowing with merriment as she continued to look around.

The house was not fancy. It was simply a classic ranch style house. Grace noted the three bedrooms. *Andrea and I will share again for sure*, Grace thought. *I will have had my fill of sleepovers by the time we go home.* She gave a little sigh. It made her uncomfortable to think that she was the only one of the three young Magicians who actually felt at home in Normality. It made sense (after all, she *had* grown up here), but it also made her feel as though she had been singled out from her friends. *Well*, she reasoned with herself, *I am a Magician. It was just my parents' decision that made me grow up here while Andrea and Tom were learning Magic in the Dimension where I really belong.*

Grace walked into the kitchen and almost laughed with delight. The cabinets were filled with dinner packets. Quickly, Tom checked all of the drawers. He found what he was looking for and shouted with glee. "Dessert!" he cried.

Grace smiled as she stood behind him. Tonight would be more like nights were at School. *Except—the Master's not here*, she realized sadly. *But*, she brightened, *we'll soon be back at the School with the Master. I'm just glad we're* here.

The thing about being in a Magical house in the Normal Dimension was that while there were Magical doors and dinners, they also had the modern pleasures of television and—as Tom soon discovered—video games. He questioned Grace about it, and she remarked with a sly smile, "It's a video game. Here, I'll show you." So while Jerra rested, Grace and the twins enjoyed fun entertainment in the form of modern electronics until dinner time.

Dinner was a merry meal that lasted all evening. The chatter was abundant, as was the food, and the children went to bed feeling full and happy.

The next morning was Thursday, and an ominous cloud seemed to hang over the house. Everyone knew, almost by instinct, that something would happen that day. They muddled through the morning activities feeling tense and distracted.

Jerra seemed to fulfill their suspicions when she handed Grace her keyring. All of the children assumed their guesses to be fact, but none of them wanted to voice their suspicions, which seemed more reliable by the minute.

Finally, Andrea whispered, "You're going to leave today, aren't you, Jerra?"

Jerra sighed and nodded. "I hate to leave you three sitting here without any guardian at all, but the Master deems it necessary. You are, after all, only teenagers, but you are also CLAIMED." She paused and sighed. "On a more cheerful note, today you will meet the newest CLAIMED, because, as you have guessed, we are getting him today."

In the brief silence that followed, Tom gave a little cheer. Everyone turned to look at him, and he turned red. "Oh, come on," he protested. "I've been the only boy at the School for years. Won't you allow me a little celebration?"

Jerra smiled, and Andrea coughed falsely to hide her giggle. Grace just stood where she was and glanced around at all of them. Her heart was heavy over the thought that she would soon be alone in the Normal Dimension.

Tom frowned at Grace's solemn face. "Why are you laughing? What's so funny?"

Grace offered a half-smile at his sarcasm. "Better?"

Tom shrugged. "You're just acting like you're going to your own funeral. It's not *that* bad that Jerra's leaving. No offense, Jerra."

"I don't know," Grace responded. "Maybe I am going to my own funeral. Remember what happened to our parents? What's to prevent that from happening to us?"

Andrea winced visibly and Tom grimaced. Jerra decided to retake control of the conversation. "Grace Maryanne Foster! Don't say that! *Nothing* like that is going to happen on this trip, do you understand? Please don't be so pessimistic."

Grace rolled her eyes. She was tired and afraid of what the rest of the journey might hold for her, and it showed.

"And don't be rude!" Jerra admonished. "Come on, guys, cheer up. *Especially* you, Grace. Just because you don't like the situation you're put in doesn't mean that you can't make the best of it. And this is not the worst situation I've ever been put in, believe me!"

The children sat stone-faced, so Jerra continued. "You three go do something. I have preparations to make before we leave this house." The children nodded. They strolled into the living room. Andrea burst into tears. Tom raised his eyebrows as if saying, *What?*

"It's just—a few days ago I was so thrilled to be here, and I know I should still be, but I'm not! I'm not happy, or thrilled, or thankful, or anything! I'm scared. I just want to go home."

Grace took a deep breath and closed her eyes. "I understand, Andrea. I really do. But we're here for a reason, remember? We can't just go home. And we can't give up, either. We just need to do the right thing and get the job done, and we'll be home before you know it."

"*Girls*," Tom huffed, rolling his eyes and leaving the room.

Andrea took a long, shaky breath and deliberately looked away from Grace. Grace frowned. "What's up? What did I do wrong?"

"You may not have ever known your parents, Grace, but I knew mine! I loved them, and they were brutally killed. You may be an orphan, but you don't really know what it's like to lose your parents! You had no right to…" Andrea burst into tears again, hiding her last words.

Grace bit her lip. Andrea was right. Grace had never gotten to know her parents. Andrea was—lucky! She had gotten to meet and to *know* her parents before they died. Grace didn't even know what her parents *looked* like. "You are *lucky*, Andrea! You're right, I never *knew* my parents. I don't even know what my parents *looked* like. I never even got to meet them when I was old enough to remember it." Grace took a deep breath and looked at her friend. Andrea frowned, her eyes furious. She stood, turned sharply on her heel, and stormed out of the room. The first tears leaked out of Grace's eyes and rolled down her face.

***

Andrea refused to speak to Grace for the rest of the morning. Grace, who had never known her friend to be sensitive or quick-tempered before, was thoroughly puzzled.

She, too, was angry, though, and she did not search for Andrea. Tom avoided them both, and Jerra, who remained in her room, was completely oblivious to the situation.

When Jerra emerged from her room at noon, she observed the children's lack of communication with a great degree of frustration. Narrowing her eyes, she took in the situation. Tom had locked himself in his room, as had Andrea, and Grace was sitting sullenly in the living room staring into space. Salty tracks ran down her cheeks from the tears that had long since dried.

Jerra frowned. She talked Grace into coming into the hall with her. Jerra marched firmly up to Andrea's door and rapped on it with her knuckles before hurrying to Tom's door to do the same. She glared at the children after the others emerged from behind their separate doors. "You are supposed to be a team, and this is the opposite of teamwork. I am going to eat. When I come back, I expect this issue will have been resolved."

Tom glanced at the others. He appeared bashful and a little afraid. After all, he had not really been part of the argument.

Andrea was the opposite. She had stopped crying, but her eyes were red and she wore upon her face an intensely pained expression. She looked like she had just stopped crying and she could start up again at any second, which was probably true.

Grace took a step backward, disturbed by her friend's look of extreme pain. Andrea's face crumpled, but she didn't cry. Tom hurried into his room and locked the door back.

"I—I'm sorry, Grace," Andrea began. "It's just— everyone has something that sets them off, and that is mine. I can't stand it if someone who never knew my parents talks about, you know—*that*—so freely."

Grace nodded. "I should be apologizing, not you. I'm just—envious that you got to know your parents. I never had that."

Andrea smiled weakly. "I know. I wish you could have." She stopped speaking because the tears were threatening again. "Oh, Grace." Her voice broke, and she stepped forward to hug her friend.

Andrea's stomach gave an enormous growl, and the girls laughed. "I guess it's time to eat?" Grace asked.

Andrea nodded. "Let's find Tom and tell him it's lunchtime."

Tom stepped out of his room. "It's alright, I already know."

They grinned and hurried down the hall.

11. Zachariah

Although it had been a strange morning, it was an isolated incident. Grace avoided speaking about that subject, for which Andrea was grateful, and Andrea was careful not to speak too much about her parents, as well.

After they finished lunch, which was a quiet meal, Jerra gathered their belongings and they left, carefully locking the door behind them. Once in Gretchen's car, Jerra began to drive north. Then east. Then south, but for less time than she had north. Then east once more.

The road was bumpy, although the highway had been smooth. It was a red gravel road, which was unusual for a capital city. Lining it on either side were many houses, some larger than others, but all in a neat row. Here and there a child was playing in a yard or on a swing. The tidy front lawns showcased the fact that the home owners were people who prized their homes and cared about the way they appeared.

Jerra slammed on the brakes. Grace's first thought was, *Are we there already? No, we can't be.* Then she realized, *That was an abrupt stop.* She then noticed the little squirrel that had run out in front of the car. *Oh,* she thought, *that's all.*

Jerra began to move forward again. Eventually Grace began to wonder if they were almost to their destination, because Jerra kept peering carefully out of the windows at the mailboxes, studying the street numbers.

Grace noted that the numbers on one side of the street did not correspond to those on the other side. (For example: 909 was opposite 918. Past 909 was 911, and past 918 was 120.) She studied the names on the boxes. Some were normal (Jones, Stewart, White, and Williams), while others were noticeably unique (Inglington, Shireford, Mileswest, and—here Grace laughed—Squash).

Jerra slowed down again as they came up to a box marked Harris, 202. Opposite it was Lexington, 193. Jerra pulled into the drive at the Harris home.

"Come on, kids. Time to meet your new classmate." The children clambered out of the car and strolled up to the door, trying to appear casual.

A tall, skinny boy with glasses and a few freckles answered the door. His nose turned up a little, which would have given him a slightly saucy appearance had it not been for the intelligence displayed in his blue eyes. His hair was light brown, and it stuck up a little in the back. "Hello?" he greeted cautiously.

"Hello." Jerra smiled. Her expression was much kinder and less business-like than it had been when she came to get Grace, as the occasion had required. "I'm Jerra Baker." She extended her hand, and the boy shook it.

Grace could almost see the electricity jump between them as they made contact. The boy's shocked eyes turned into a pale green. He rung his hand out and shook his head as if trying to remove water from his ears.

But other than that, his reaction was quite different from Grace's. His eyes were confused, but he remained polite. "Nice to meet you, Ms. Baker. And these are…?" He gestured at the three teenagers.

As Jerra introduced the children, Grace wondered that he had not been more puzzled over the electricity and the fact that his mind was now tingling with alertness. She was sure his mind was. Then the simple truth hit her: he had been raised to be polite, and Grace had not been. He was curious, but it might seem rude to ask.

The boy spoke again. "My name is Zachariah Goldwyn."

"Good to meet you, Zachariah," the twins chorused.

Grace remained silent. Jerra looked towards the girl pointedly as a mischievous smile began to spread across Grace's face. "The static electricity *sure* is bad here," Grace stated, putting on her best Southern accent, which sounded very unconvincing. Zachariah only appeared all the more confused. "This static seems to go right up into your mind. Of *course*, you're used to it, but all of us are not." Jerra glared at Grace, but Andrea and Tom were beginning to giggle. "I wonder why it is so crazily static up here, y'all," she concluded.

Zachariah smiled tensely, the smile not reaching his eyes. The other children could tell he was wondering what was going on. "Well," he finally replied. "Very nice to meet you, but I really do need to finish my work. Homeschooling, you know." He smiled apologetically.

Jerra shook her head. "No, you don't. I," she broke the ice, "am a Magician. So are these two girls. He," she pointed at Tom, "is a wizard. And so are *you*."

Zachariah rapidly tried to back into the house, but he found his way blocked by an invisible barrier. "Who are you?" he asked, narrowing his eyes in suspicion. "What do you want?"

Jerra looked at him. "Look, Zach. You aren't supposed to be here. Charles and Lillian were Magicians, too, you know."

Zachariah gave a strangled gasp. "How do you know my parents' names? And don't call me Zach!"

Grace put in, "I'm an orphan, too. I was in an orphanage in New York until a few months ago, when Jerra got me. Now..." She raised her hand, and a wind stirred the leaves close to Zachariah's feet. Jerra raised her eyebrows but didn't comment.

"Okay, okay," Zachariah responded. "I get it. We're all Magical. So what?"

"Come with us, Zachariah," pleaded Tom. "I've been the only boy at the School for years. If you come, I won't be alone anymore. *And* we'll be learning Magic."

Zachariah was puzzled. These people were telling the truth. That much was obvious in their manner, their speech, and their actions. But it was strange—they wanted him to just leave. What would his foster parents say? Did these people think his foster parents just wouldn't notice he'd left?

On the other hand, Zachariah wanted to go. He was immensely intrigued by the idea of Magic and its use. "I don't know," he answered finally. "I want to go. But—I live here! The other people who live here will freak out. They'll think I've disappeared! I can't just—go!"

"Oh, yes." Jerra sounded perfectly at ease. She was forcing his hand, and she knew it. "That always seems like such a big problem, doesn't it? It befuddled Grace, too. But no fear! They will not worry. They will not remember you at all. In fact, they have already forgotten. All the people that you have ever known have forgotten."

The boy inhaled sharply and narrowed his eyes, but Jerra's last announcement had made it impossible for him to turn her down. Besides, he couldn't get back inside. He did not doubt the Magician's word for a second. "Alright," he responded. "Take me with you."

Jerra turned to the other three children. "This is where we part ways. We—" she pointed to herself and Zachariah "—are driving back to New York to give Gretchen her car back because, of course, none of you can drive. Zachariah and I will head back to the School. You three will have to walk. I am sorry, but there is no other way. Use the map of parallel Magical houses and the keyring that goes with it whenever possible, and use your Magic to your advantage. Be safe. I will see you soon." With a tight smile, she gave each of them a small hug and handed Grace yet another scroll. She and Zachariah walked to the car and were gone.

"Well." Grace broke the silence when the car had disappeared from view. "I have to admit that this is the strangest situation I've ever been in."

Tom and Andrea stood silently, looking expectantly at Grace. Grace slowly unrolled the scroll and they all studied it together. Grace smiled. "That," she remarked, "makes perfect sense."

It was a map of the United States, with a number here and there on it, each of which pinpointed a Magically owned house. The numbers on the map corresponded to those on the keys. Grace's heart swelled with immense gratitude when she saw number thirty-seven on the map. She grinned. Number thirty-seven: 193 Breezy Road, Hartford, Connecticut.

It was across the street.

12. House of Secrets

Grace felt relief sweep over her in a whoosh. It did not take long for the three exhausted teenagers to hurry across the narrow road, although it did take a minute for Grace to find key number thirty-seven. The children tumbled through the doorway and locked it securely behind them. Grace took a deep breath and leaned against the door. She was too tired to even notice the grandeur of the house.

Through unspoken consent, they each went into their separate rooms. Grace sat down in a chair by her window with a sigh. The adventure was really only beginning, that she knew for sure.

Andrea wandered down the hall into a room lined with shelves. *A library,* she thought, eagerly breathing in the scent of the old books. She curled up in a chair in a corner with a book titled *The High Enchanted*. With a sigh of pleasure, she lost herself in the Magic of its old, handwritten pages.

Tom had fallen in a posture of pure exhaustion on the couch. He rolled over and closed his eyes. It was not long before he dozed off.

The large clock in the kitchen began to chime, and Grace started awake. She smiled, although with no real humor. She was just too tired to even sit down without drifting off. Her stomach grumbled loudly, so she decided to get something to eat.

Grace hurried down the hall into the kitchen. The five chimes had rolled through the house like thunder, so she was surprised to see Tom still asleep when she passed by the living room. She snorted. *Boys sleep like rocks*, she thought scornfully. She continued on her way to the kitchen.

It cheered Grace to see the cabinets full of dinner packets and dessert packets. It made her feel like she was still in the Magic Dimension. She did not eat any of the dinner packets, however. Instead, she opened the pantry and poured a handful of peanuts into a waiting bowl. She finished consuming them, so she decided to explore the house.

It was a strange house, much larger and more complicated than the one they had stayed in the previous night. The wide hallway at the front of the house was made spectacularly, with high ceilings and wooden floors. Grace hesitated a moment before walking down to the room at the opposite end of the hallway. The door to the room towered majestically above her. *It's almost like someone disguised a castle to look like a house from the outside*, Grace thought in awe.

The door opened before her, as in most Magical buildings, and she found herself in the library. She tiptoed around, knowing she could stay in here for weeks or even months and still not finish reading every book. She jumped as she went around a corner. Then she breathed a sigh of relief as she realized it was only Andrea, who had fallen asleep. Grace smiled and continued examining the shelves.

When she was bored looking at the old titles of Magic books, Grace left the library. The door closest to her opened, and she found herself in a bedroom. She continued through the hall and discovered that the next two doors also led to bedrooms.

After she passed these, she came to the living room. The long sofas sat snugly against the walls, while the television stood on a low table at one end of the room. It a corner stood a coffee table with a small lamp on it. Tom lay on one of the couches, sleeping. Grace grinned. *If I were to actually live here, I would be quite comfortable. This is such a neat, clean, cozy little house.*

After exiting the living room, there was only one more door at the end of the hallway. This, as Grace knew, was the kitchen.

Grace was about to turn around and head back to the library when she noticed something strange. It was on the wall beside the living room. Grace looked closer. Her eyes widened. *A door knob?*

It wasn't a Magical door, so it did not open on its own, but Grace seized the knob, turned, and pulled. The door, which had so perfectly blended into the wall, opened easily, and Grace stepped into a narrow passageway. The passageway was hardly two feet wide but extended about ten feet before Grace reached another door, which opened without trouble like the first. Grace entered a hallway, perpendicular to the passageway, and shut the door behind herself.

The hallway lay before Grace, about as long as the hallway in the front part of the house but not as wide. Along the floor ran a soft, woven red carpet. This hallway, also like the front one, was lined with doors. Grace opened the nearest door. It seemed that the back part of the house did not have Magical doorways.

The room that Grace entered was relatively large compared to the other rooms she had visited so far. It was about the size of the library and a bedroom combined. The size was not the thing that most struck Grace, though. The walls had been covered in pictures, and photo albums lay in stacks on a long table at the other end of the room. As Grace studied the pictures, she realized that they were portraits of young couples and families. In the pictures, the people were depicted smiling and laughing. Their joy showed in their faces, as did the love and respect that they had for one another.

Who are these people? Grace wondered, noting that the portraits were not all of the same family but instead depicted several different laughing couples and families. There were about fifty different pictures on the walls, lined up to be displayed. *Who are they, and why are they here?* Grace mentally asked to no one in particular.

Grace walked slowly to the back of the room, where the long table stood with all of the albums. The stacks were tall and there were many of them. She guessed that there were about three times as many albums as there were portraits. Grace pulled a random album down from the shelf.

It, too, was filled with images of laughter and joy, but all of the photos in this album were of the same family. Grace turned the pages softly. There were wedding photos and pictures of the family at home. There were images of the family visiting with friends at home and at events.

Grace reached up and slid the album back into place. She pulled down a second album and turned through its pages with gentle fingers. The smiles of fun at Christmastime and on birthdays seemed to pop off of the pages. Grace sighed in contentment. Something about looking at the cheerful people made her happy, too.

Grace set the second album aside and pulled down another. The pictures fascinated her. She wondered why they were all piled up here instead of at the homes of the people depicted, why they were here, and not being shared and laughed over.

Grace pulled down a fourth album. She set it on her knee and let it fall open over her lap. She grinned with the young couple depicted on the pages. They looked so happy and carefree. Grace felt strangely attached to this couple in particular. She studied their faces. The faces looked familiar, but she couldn't tell where she knew them from. *How would I know a Magical family, anyway? Besides the Burlingtons, of course*, she reasoned. *I must just be imagining the familiarity.*

Grace turned the page. Her jaw dropped in recognition. In the photo, the couple was standing at the door of a house with another couple. Both of the mothers were pregnant in the image, but the woman who was not familiar to Grace was more obviously so.

It was the house that Grace recognized first. She had only seen it in one place before, but she remembered the structure with perfect clarity. The only time she had seen the house was on the wall of Andrea's room. At the School, the house was in the background of a picture of Andrea, Tom, and their parents. Grace narrowed her eyes, studying the photo. Yes, the two who Grace had not recognized were definitely Tom and Andrea's parents, and they were standing in front of their house with two people who looked remarkably familiar to Grace.

Realization dawned on Grace and she touched the picture gently. She knew why they looked so familiar—she saw them every day when she looked in the mirror. "Mom?" she whispered softly. "Dad?"

The clock chimed. It sounded distant and far away, but it cut through the silence like a knife. Grace counted the chimes. She was shocked to count seven before the clock quieted. She bit her lip and looked back at the album with longing.

Grace set the album that contained the pictures of her parents to one side, away from all of the others. With a sigh of regret, she stood, knowing that her friends would be concerned about where she was. *I'll come back*, she told herself firmly. *I'll come look in here tomorrow, too.*

As she stepped into the hall, she glanced down towards the other end. She hadn't explored any of the other rooms. *Oh, well.* Grace smiled. *The others can come with me tomorrow.* She hurried down the narrow passageway into the front hallway.

The hallway was deserted. Grace could hear someone rustling around in the kitchen. *Probably Tom*, she guessed. From the library she could hear Andrea calling her name. *Yep, Tom's in the kitchen*, Grace confirmed mentally.

Grace turned and ran towards the library. "Andrea, I'm here!" she cried.

Andrea burst out of the library and ran smack into Grace. She gave Grace an enormous, enthusiastic hug. "Where were you? I've been searching for over an *hour!*"

"It's—rather difficult to explain. I know you were scared, and I'm sorry," Grace replied quietly. Andrea looked at Grace suspiciously, but Grace continued. "I'll show you where I was, but wait until tomorrow. I will need you to help me explore the rest of it, after all."

Andrea's eyes were bright with curiosity, but she did not press Grace for more information. "Alright," she agreed.

Grace smiled at her, her eyes shining with gratitude. "Thank you."

***

Grace knew that they needed to leave to continue with their mission, but she could not resist showing Andrea and Tom her discovery, not to mention the other rooms. Thus Grace proposed that they leave in the early afternoon, after she had showed them what she had found and after they had conducted further explorations. The twins agreed to her proposal, albeit reluctantly.

They grew more excited as time wore on, however. By the time they had finished breakfast and gotten ready the next day, they were fairly dancing with curiosity.

Grace led them to the hidden doorknob. Andrea gasped as Grace opened the door, but Tom merely nodded. "Go on," he instructed. Grace gently opened the door to the room full of pictures. The trio stepped inside.

The twins looked around quietly, but their expressions bore only the curiosity that Grace had had upon first entering the room. Andrea leaned closer to the portraits. "This is really cool, Grace. I wonder why their all piled up here, and not at these peoples' homes?"

"I don't know." Grace shrugged. "That, uh, wasn't really what I wanted to show you, though." She hurried to the album where it lay in the back of the room. She let it fall open on her knee before she sat down on the floor with a sigh. Andrea and Tom plopped down on either side of her.

"Grace?" Andrea questioned, puzzled. "What is it you wanted to show us, exactly?"

Grace held up the book. "Do these people look at all familiar to you? At *all*? Do they remind you of someone, perhaps?"

Andrea shook her head. Tom, on the other hand, had realization dawning on his face. He looked at Grace, his eyes shining in wonder. "Yes. They look like—"

"Hush!" Grace cried. "Let Andrea figure it out for herself." Andrea still looked lost, so Grace flipped to the page that showed Andrea's parents. She knew it was cruel, but she wondered if it would help Andrea make the connection. It had helped Grace, after all.

Andrea gave a strangled little gasp. "That's my parents! And our house! But I still..." She shook her head in confusion.

Grace held up her hand and gestured to Tom. "What do you think? You look like you have a guess."

"They're your parents!" Tom supplied. "They are, for sure. Don't you see how much they resemble Grace,

98

Andrea? And they were visiting our parents at our house. See, our mom was pregnant with us, and Grace's mom was pregnant with her. They *have* to be your parents, Grace."

Grace nodded, smiling. "That's my guess, too. It makes perfect sense, doesn't it?" She looked at Andrea for support.

Andrea nodded with her. "Yes, of course. It *does* make sense. But why is it here?"

Grace shrugged, at a loss. "I honestly have no idea. Once I found this, I couldn't tear myself away. It's—it's the first time I've actually seen my parents before. I've imagined them, yes. But I've never actually—" Her voice broke, and she looked down.

Andrea put a hand on Grace's shoulder. She decided to change the subject. "What's in all those other rooms? There sure are plenty of them."

"I don't know. I didn't have time to explore them," Grace answered, glancing up. "Do you want to?"

"Yes!" cried the twins simultaneously.

The trio laughed as they stood. Grace regretfully put the album back, although she set it away from the others. She wanted to be able to find it easily if she ever came back. With an inaudible sigh, she followed her friends back into the hall.

The back of the house, it seemed, was made for mysteries. The next room that the children entered was full of scrolls and old books—or, more accurately, ancient books. There were piles of scrolls on one shelf, stacks of books on another, and rows of blank paper on the last shelf. In the center of the room was a large table upon which were more books. One lay open in front of the only chair in the room. Alongside the book sat a thick stack of paper. Tom snorted as he noticed the quill pen. It seemed strange to see the quaint object in the normal Dimension. Grace leaned closer to study the book.

Grace immediately noticed that it was not written in English. *In tisi casem, omn magei es unzeifcunt opposi et poket is milus*, she read to herself. *Oh!* she realized. *It's a translation!* Grace was about to mention this to her friends when she heard a shout of surprise from behind her. She whirled around and witnessed Andrea shaking out her hand with a dazed expression on her face.

What had happened was this: Andrea had been examining the old parchment on a shelf when her hand had brushed against a blank piece. It had immediately crumpled into dust. Andrea breathed a sigh of relief, glad that it had been blank. "Let's go into the next room," she gasped. "We could mess something up in here." The other teenagers took her advice.

The next two rooms were not, by any of the teenagers' definitions, very special or interesting at all. They were simple bedrooms, not unlike the ones located in the front of the house. The children could only guess that they had been hidden in the back because the people who had once slept in them could not bear to be parted from their Magical rooms.

The next room was, to be sure, quite intriguing. The first thing that struck Grace was the fact that the room closely resembled a preschool. The tables were low and the chairs small, hinting that the room had been mainly used by little ones. This was revealed to be a fact when the children opened the cabinets and discovered books with simple words and lots of pictures, books about basic Magic.

"Homeschool," Andrea observed. "Homeschool of young Magicians. In fact, I bet the little scholars would have been in preschool or kindergarten, had they been in a regular, non-Magical school."

Grace couldn't hide the grin that swept across her face. "Of course. Magical homeschool—I wouldn't have guessed it. It's such a preposterous idea—and yet, when I think about it, it is really quite logical."

Tom shrugged. "It's just ridiculous to you because you've never thought about it. It's actually more common than you might think."

Even Tom's sensible words could not wipe the smile off Grace's face. She shook her head, trying to process the idea. It was true—she *had* never considered it before. She had never even *thought* to consider it before. It had just simply not occurred to her that some Magicians might homeschool, as well. And yet—it made so much sense.

Andrea fiddled with the doorknob. "Do you want to go on? We need to leave here as soon as possible to continue on our journey, so we really need to get going if we are going to finish exploring all these rooms."

"Chill, Andy," remarked Tom, who was trying to squeeze into one of the itty-bitty chairs. "We have all morning."

The clock chimed eleven, punctuating Andrea's point. She turned beseeching eyes on Grace. Grace nodded. "Andrea's right. Even though there is only one more room,

101

we still need to get going. We should leave here by twelve-thirty at the latest, and we still have to pack up."

Tom rolled his eyes but tried to stand up. He had some trouble removing himself from the tiny chair, but with the girls' help he managed it. They exited the room quietly and strode towards the final door.

Grace opened it. The smell that wafted out hit the children's nostrils with the force of a small truck, making them cough. It smelled absolutely despicable—a mixture of rotten eggs and sour milk. The children scrambled away from the door.

"What is that?" Grace choked, her voice sounding squeaky because she was pinching her nose.

Tom squeezed his nose and peered inside. "It's, like, a pharmacy, or something. I'm not really sure—but there's a bunch of bottles and stuff."

Andrea snorted at his terminology and then gagged as the stench filled her nose. "It's an apothecary, not a pharmacy. It's filled with potion ingredients," she explained.

Grace nodded and held her breath so she could look around. Andrea was right. High shelves lined the walls. Above them were bright lights, but the shelves themselves cast formidable shadows on the floor. Atop the shelves sat numerous jars that appeared to have once been large pickle jars, but had been kept back here for storage of some—other things. Each jar contained a different substance, ranging in color from pitch black to scarlet to shimmering silver.

The jars were all labeled. Grace read a few of the labels silently. *Bat's teeth, lizard's tails, snail slime.* Grace grimaced. No wonder the room stunk. She scanned the next few labels and then stared at them in astonishment. *Unicorn tail strands, naiad scales, dragon blood.* Her brain seemed to bounce around inside her skull. Unicorns? Naiads? *Dragons?* Her lungs burned for air, so she stepped out of the room.

She raised an eyebrow at Andrea. "Naiads? Dragons? Unicorns?" she panted.

Andrea's green eyes sparkled with mirth. "Of course." She paused, smiling. "Why Magic and no Magical creatures? Although, of course, they exist only in the Magical Dimension. I have never seen a unicorn or a dragon, but I have seen a naiad once. When I was little..." she trailed off, lost in thought.

Tom had remained silent throughout this dialogue, but now he spoke up. "Why are we just standing here? I thought we were on a *schedule*." His voice dripped with sarcasm on the last word.

Grace, however, chose to ignore the sarcasm. "He's right. We finished exploring the hallway, didn't we? We should be getting ready to leave, not just 'standing here,' to quote Tom."

Andrea nodded, and the twins slowly followed Grace up the hall back to the front of the house.

13. Against the Elements

Grace solemnly locked the door with the key numbered thirty-seven. She felt miserable about leaving the album with her parents' pictures, but she knew that it would be stealing to take it. With a sigh, she turned away from the house and towards her waiting friends.

They consulted the map of where the CLAIMED were located. The next star that marked the home of someone who was CLAIMED lay in the upper part of Maine in a tiny little town called Frenchville.

Tom lifted his finger and pointed down the road. "We need to go that way." He began to trudge in the indicated direction, shifting his backpack as he did so.

"How do you know that?" queried Andrea, stepping swiftly beside him. Grace followed behind her.

"This is north," Tom replied sullenly. "And we need to head north." He rolled his eyes as though the answer were obvious and as if anyone with a brain should know the answer without even asking.

"He's right," Grace remarked, gesturing up towards the sky.

"Alright," Andrea responded quietly, giving in. "Lead the way, friends who understand directions." She smiled dryly.

Grace stepped firmly and confidently to the front of the group. She headed briskly in a northeasterly direction.

Travelling was much slower going without a car. It was also much more tiring. Grace slumped, discouraged, when they stopped at 4:30 at house number seventy-two. They had only travelled twenty-three miles that day. She tried to locate the key on Jerra's keyring. The many keys were in no order at all, and she was surprised that she managed to find it after only five minutes. The three children hurried into the house and closed the door.

There was nothing unusual or mysterious about house number seventy-two. It was a nice house, well made and well decorated, clean and comfortable, but with no secrets or surprises hidden behind unknown doors. The time spent there was enjoyable, even if it was not very memorable.

The next morning did not exceed Grace's expectations in any way. Even though the children got an early start, the gray clouds that were gathering in the sky threatened to let lose torrents of rain at any second. The children were hesitant to depart in such unpromising weather, but, as Grace reasoned, they needed to use any time that they had to put some distance behind them. Thus the children departed the house and began to travel once more towards Frenchville, albeit with some misgivings.

It was mid-morning when the bottom dropped out of the heavens. The downpour came so suddenly that the children were instantly drenched. They scrambled for the relative cover of the nearby trees.

The children knew that there was a great risk in doing this and that it was considered just plain idiotic to go under trees during a rainstorm. However, though the winds raged not fifty feet from where they stood, all around the children the only rustle was caused by their own feet and hands atop the leaves and twigs.

The little clump of trees pleased Grace immensely. There were not too many trees, so as to crowd around the children and make them uncomfortable. Nor were there too few, so as to leave the children completely exposed to the elements. There were just the right amount for both security and relative comfort. Above the children, also, there was the perfect amount of branches, woven together in the perfect way, to shield the children from the rain as best as possible, considering the circumstances.

Not that the children were comfortable. Tom was noticeably muddy (although he did not seem too put out by this—he seemed to enjoy the dirt), and he was soaked to the skin. Grace sat shivering and wrung out her drenching hair. Andrea, too, was shivering with cold and fright, although she did not seem to be as wet as the rest of them. Altogether, they were a group of cold, dirty, soaked children, who all wished that they were back at house number seventy-two.

Gradually the downpour subsided, although a steady drizzle continued. The constant dripping of the rain served to make the children even more miserable, for there was no way to get dry while the rain continued. Finally, the small group tentatively emerged from their hiding place and began to hike onwards, marching to the sound of trickling water falling down off the trees.

By the time the children stopped for the night at house number thirteen, all three of the children were hungry and ill-tempered. They had only travelled a total of thirty miles, it was seven-thirty in the evening, and it had not been the most pleasant day of their adventure. They each took a shower, ate dinner in despairing silence, and went to bed.

The next morning did not look any more promising than the day prior. None of the teenagers wanted to leave, but they knew that they had to make it to Frenchville, rain or shine. They courageously set out for their destination yet again, with set jaws and firm determination. Grace led the way out into the gloomy weather.

This time it was almost noon before the rain came pouring down. The children huddled once more under the trees, waiting for the downpour to stop. And yet again, the winds did not harm the children and the trees sheltered them. Not that this made them feel thankful. They simply wished that the storm would cease, the clouds would part, and the sun would shine again. It was not to be so.

The downpour's calming announced the children's departure from the trees. They marched firmly down the road, not talking, just concentrating on making it to the next house. They had not made much progress today, either.

This weather continued for the next three days. Grace hardly noticed the fact that they had been in the Normal Dimension for a week. The strange thing was that the winds never endangered the children by raging above their shelter, and the rain did not pour down if they were far from a clump of trees. The children brushed this off as mere coincidence.

By Thursday, they were in the middle of Maine. They knew that they would be able to move more quickly now that the bad weather was over. Grace only hoped that they would reach Frenchville in the next couple of days, since they could travel faster now.

Her wish was not to be granted.

14. Alongside the Elements

Thursday took the record for the strangest day so far. Grace awoke in her tiny bedroom off the side of the living room in house number ninety-one. She could hear Andrea rolling around on the bunk underneath her. She groggily sat up before pushing off the bed with her arms and jumping down onto the floor from the top bunk.

House number ninety-one was the smallest house they had visited so far. It consisted solely of a small kitchen with a tiny pantry leading off it, a living room, and two bedrooms, each of which contained a bunkbed and an itty-bitty clothes chest. Tom had joked that the house must have been made for dwarves; everything in it was so small.

The door into the living room opened itself for Grace. The house was still Magical, despite its size.

Grace ate her breakfast quickly and packed her things before setting her bag by the door. Today would be a wonderful day for travelling—it was sunny and the children would get an early start.

They set out at a brisk pace. The day was bright and cheerful, and they could hear birds singing in the trees. Still, Grace could not ignore the sense of foreboding in her mind. She tried to shake off the feeling, but she couldn't. She jumped when Andrea gave a small sigh.

Andrea turned to her friend. "What's up? You're acting really strange. What's bothering you?"

Grace shook her head. "Nothing. I'm just ready to get to Frenchville already." She smiled weakly, but she stomped on the ground, portraying her true feelings. Dust rose up in small clouds around her ankles, covering her shoes in dirt.

Andrea narrowed her eyes with suspicion. "That's not true, and you know it. Something *is* bothering you, but you don't want to tell me because you're afraid it's something bad. Is that right?" She studied her friend with innocent but searching eyes.

"No! No, it's not," Grace protested. She shook her head, wishing her brain would tell her more. "Just—don't talk to me right now, okay?"

Andrea frowned. She knew it was not like Grace to act like this, and she knew it was not like Grace to hide something of importance. She could also tell that Grace was apprehensive and a little frightened, which scared Andrea. Grace was not easily frightened.

Tom strolled behind them obliviously. The good thing about the girls not trusting him with any important information was just that—he never had to worry about any important information. This, as he knew, was both good and bad—while he never had to worry, he never got to know about any problems or give possible solutions to the aforesaid problems. Nonetheless, he was perfectly fine with letting them do that while he relaxed. Or, not relaxed, since they were walking, but he got to walk quietly in the back. He whistled a tune in calm oblivion.

Andrea slowed her step so that she fell behind Grace in the line. She sighed audibly, worried. Tom rolled his eyes. *Girls. Always so dramatic*, he complained mentally. *They should just* relax.

110

Something weird was happening to Grace. She was positive that something was going to happen that day. Earlier she had thought it would be a bad something. Now, she wasn't so sure. The something only felt mysterious, but not dangerous. *Or I'm going crazy*, Grace thought. *I can't know anything. But I do!* She, too, gave an audible sigh. Tom rolled his eyes in annoyance. *What are the girls fussing about, anyway?* he thought.

Andrea sensed the change in her friend's mood. (She was one of those rare and wonderful people who could tell exactly how someone was feeling by their expression and posture alone.) She frowned, wondering at the change, but she knew Grace would only evade her questions again if she asked, so she remained silent.

Grace knew that Andrea was frustrated with her lack of communication. *I can't tell her anything, though*, she reasoned. *I don't know anything myself.* She frowned thoughtfully, wondering what to do, but feeling that things would explain themselves to both her and Andrea in due time.

She was right. She would find out, and so would Andrea.

Grace strode along quickly, annoyed that she could not determine her own thoughts. What was getting into her? She couldn't even communicate with her best friend. She absentmindedly kicked at the dirt.

Tom watched the dirt around Grace's feet as though he was in a trance. He felt something odd going on in his mind as he observed, like a switch was being turned on inside his brain. He lifted his hands and stared at them. He

111

raised them, and he felt the switch in his mind turn all the way on. He felt for the dirt, and he willed it to come and stick to his hands like a magnet. The dust rose up together and stuck to his hands in a clump. Tom glanced up at the girls guiltily. The Master had warned them against using Magic unless they had to, and this was hardly an emergency. He brushed the dirt off his hands, hoping the girls had not noticed.

While Tom had been magnetizing dirt, Andrea was staring with frustration at the back of Grace's neck. The day was hot, and sweat beaded both Andrea's forehead and Grace's neck. Andrea frowned. She was frustrated, puzzled, and confused. What did Grace know that she was refusing to share with anyone else? And *how* did she know it? Andrea glared at the droplets of sweat. Without realizing it, Andrea raised her hands. The water droplets formed a solid drop that flew into Andrea's outstretched hand. Andrea's eyes flew open as she watched, mesmerized. Once the droplet reached her palm, the water held its shape instead of puddling in her hand. Andrea shook her hand out, and the ball of liquid fell into the dust and disappeared. Andrea's mouth flew open in astonishment, but she quickly shut it and kept walking.

Grace had not noticed the moisture leaving her neck. While Tom had been playing with dirt and Andrea toying with water, Grace was involved in her own mystery.

Grace knew that something was going to happen. The closer it got to the time when it was going to occur, the more Grace new about it. About five minutes prior, Grace could tell a good deal about it. It had to do with all three of the friends, and it had to do with each of their minds. It was a talent—a talent they had been born with, but a talent that they had not known existed. It would be a discovery, of sorts—but it had nothing to do with true Magic. It had rarely happened to anyone before, and it would rarely happen to anyone ever again. Grace had no idea how she knew this. It was like someone was planting the information inside of head, instead of her thinking it.

Grace exhaled. She had been concentrating so hard that she had not realized that she was very hot. She stuck her bottom lip out and blew her hair out of her eyes. The brief gust of air did not help very much, so Grace pushed the hair out of her face with her hand. As her hand fell back down, she felt an overwhelming desire for a cooling wind to blow around her and her friends, relieving them from the intense heat.

A soft wind came down from the same direction as her hand. It blew around her and the twins, refreshing them. Grace took a deep breath of the cool air, feeling rejuvenated. The gust disappeared as soon as it had come.

Grace bit her lip, feeling guilty, and wondered if the twins had noticed. They had not, because they were too occupied with the fact that they, also, had performed Magic when it was not an emergency.

But Grace knew something that the twins didn't. She knew that this—what they had done—was not Magic. Grace recalled something that she had read in one of her books. *Manipulation of the Elements: Manipulation of fire, air, water and living earth is not considered Magic. Although it could be considered either a Charm or a Spell, it is neither, because no Magician can significantly control an element in that way. Also, the elements are not living, and their manipulation would probably not use words, so it is neither a Charm nor a Spell. Intermediate Magic uses words with living things, so it is not that either. Manipulation of the elements has never been done before, and I personally doubt it ever will be.* Grace gave a little gasp. She and her friends had done the impossible.

The brief gust of wind had long since gone, and Grace was greatly tempted to gather another. She resisted the temptation, though, because even though it wasn't Magic, it would still be highly questionable to non-Magicians. And it would be even more questionable to Magicians. How could three young CLAIMED do something that people had been unable to do for centuries? Grace frowned and shook her head in amazement.

She and the twins continued down the road, puzzling over their dilemma.

***

The children arrived at house number twenty-two in the late afternoon. They took turns in the shower and went to their separate rooms. As always, they were exhausted in the evening and did not feel like talking to one another. They stayed apart and ate supper in shifts before going to bed. It was long before any of them fell asleep, however.

Grace lay on her bed and stared up at the ceiling. The blades of the non-Magical, electronic fan whizzed around rapidly. Staring at them made Grace dizzy, but she stared at them anyway, trying not think about anything, but unable to keep her mind off of their discovery. She did not understand it, but she knew by instinct that it was important.

Grace wondered if her friends understood its significance. They probably just thought that they had used Magic without caution in the Normal Dimension, and without realizing they were doing anything until after it was over. *They* probably didn't know that it was not Magic. *They* did not understand that it was completely unheard of. *They* didn't know that it had never been done before and that it was impossible for them to have manipulated the elements. And yet they had. Grace sighed with confusion.

It almost made Grace laugh, the way life had taken her down such an unexpected road. Only two months ago she had been in a lonely orphanage with no friends and no hope. Back then, she would have laughed at the idea of Magic. Now, though, she was a young Magician, full of promise, who had just discovered that she and her friends had remarkable powers. Grace couldn't have been more surprised at the unexpected course her life had taken.

Grace rolled off her bed and her feet hit the floor. She couldn't sleep, and she needed to talk to someone. Also, Andrea and Tom needed to know the significance of what they had done today. It was time to have a conversation with her friends about the discovery of the day, and there was no better time than at that moment.

Grace knocked on each of her friends' doors as she passed. She briefly instructed them to come to the living room before she strode quickly in that direction herself. She marched into the room and sat down hard on the couch, her mind still buzzing with her discovery.

The door flew open and Andrea entered the room. She smiled at Grace. "You wanted to talk?"

"Yes, but wait. Tom will be here in just a second. He needs to be here, too," Grace answered, glanced at the door expectantly.

Andrea nodded, her wavy blond hair bouncing. She had the unique talent of being quiet without making the silence oppressive. Grace appreciated this. Together they sat and waited for Andrea's twin.

Tom entered slowly after the girls had been sitting in silence for about five minutes. He slumped into a chair, his face betraying his exhaustion. Grace wondered if he had been carelessly practicing his new talent or if it had just been a long day on the road and he felt overwhelmed. He collapsed with his head in his hands and glanced at Grace with a weary expression.

Grace took this as a cue to begin. She looked at her friends calculatingly before she plunged in. "Today, on the road, we all three practiced unintentional Magic." She looked at them sharply, hoping her senses had not led her astray. "Is that correct?" She studied their faces for a sign of confusion.

Andrea nodded slowly. "Yes. But how do you know that? Did you just feel it? Is that what you were all worried about this morning?"

Grace ignored her query and turned to face Tom. "You?" she questioned simply.

Tom nodded reluctantly. "Uh-huh. Why?"

116

Grace smiled at her friends' confirmation. She had been correct. "That's what I thought you'd say. But it wasn't really Magic you were doing." Grace recited the paragraph from the book that she had read.

"Cool," responded Tom with mild interest.

Andrea did not answer. She narrowed her eyes at Grace with suspicion. Grace *couldn't* have known about that beforehand, but she had. How had she known? Andrea studied Grace with inquisitive eyes, but Grace was oblivious.

Grace grinned. "It's impossible, but we did it. What a story! But—do you think we should tell anyone? It's quite a secret."

The twins shook their heads. "No," Tom replied. "Most people would just think we were lying."

Grace nodded. She liked the idea of keeping it a secret. Then she raised her eyebrows. She realized she was leaving out a critical detail. "Which elements do you two control?" she inquired.

Tom spoke up. "I'm earth. Dirt, you know."

Grace frowned, wondering if she should ask the question that was resting on the tip of her tongue. "Did you—I mean, were you practicing?"

Tom blushed and nodded. "Yeah. But I couldn't manipulate any of the other elements. I could only do stuff with earth. Water, air, and fire—they were impossible." He shrugged.

"Oh," Grace responded. "I'm air. I haven't tried anything else—" she glared with accusation at Tom "—but air just came naturally."

117

Andrea gave a little sigh and joined the conversation. "Water."

Tom stared at her, uncomprehending. "You're thirsty? We're talking about what is possibly the most revolutionary discovery in Magical history, and you feel the need to announce that you're thirsty? Really?"

Andrea rolled her eyes. "*No*. I control water, silly."

"Oh," replied Tom, looking a little ashamed of himself, but not feeling the need to apologize. He looked back at Grace, purposefully avoiding Andrea's eyes.

Grace remained silent. The twins did not realize how preposterous their situation was. They were arguing about pointless misunderstandings. Grace frowned and stood. "I just thought you two would like to know," she announced stiffly. "I'm tired. I'm going back to bed." She left the room, shaking her head as she went.

Andrea followed her out, trying to catch her while Tom was in another room. Tom sensed what she was up to and obliged by staying in the living room. It was his way of making up for the unnecessary argument.

Grace froze when she heard footsteps behind her. Guessing that they belonged to Andrea, she hesitantly turned around and studied her friend with searching eyes. "Why did you follow me?" she asked.

Andrea looked at her curiously, but not accusingly. "You knew that this would happen, didn't you? This is what you wouldn't tell me about this morning. And you knew when it happened, too. How, though?"

Grace shrugged. "I have no idea. It was honestly like someone else was putting thoughts into my head instead of me thinking them. It's as much of a mystery to me as it is to you."

Andrea could tell by Grace's expression that this was true. "Oh," she responded quietly. She sounded disappointed at the unexciting answer, but she tried to hide this behind her smile. She glanced at Grace, expecting her to continue.

Instead, Grace began to walk back to her room. She hoped that Andrea would take the hint and leave, but no.

"Grace?" Andrea began. "I don't know about you, but I'm tired of travelling. So is Tom—you saw him in there a minute ago. What would you say to us staying here a few days and resting? We can leave on Monday."

Grace turned around sharply. "But that is three whole days of not doing anything! We're here in this Dimension to gather the CLAIMED, not just to take a vacation. That is not the purpose of this trip!"

"I know. But we can't successfully complete our mission if we are constantly exhausted. You're tired, too. I can tell." Andrea winced as her sentence completed itself in her brain. *I can tell because you're so grumpy.* She shook her head to clear it of the judgmental thought. *I'm grumpy, too,* she remembered, *not just Grace. We all need a break.*

To Andrea's surprise, Grace nodded. "You're right. We do need to rest. I don't like it at all, but it is necessary. We'll leave Monday."

Andrea gave Grace a huge grin. "*Thank* you!"

Grace smiled back. "Sure thing." She turned around on her heel and marched off to her bedroom. This time, Andrea did not follow her.

15. Dawn

The three whole days of not going anywhere were good for the children. By the time that the weekend was over, they were refreshed and relaxed, having played with one another all weekend. It was Monday morning, and they felt rested and cheerful, ready to be back on the road towards Frenchville.

They had been in Normality for two whole weeks. It seemed strange to Grace that it had been fourteen days since they had departed from the Magic Dimension. It seemed to her that they had just left a few days ago, but it also felt like it had been forever since she had last seen the Master and Jerra.

The little party set out, refreshed and optimistic from their weekend of healthy rest. Grace ambitiously planned to reach their destination by Wednesday, where Tom would Initiate the new CLAIMED's Magic. Tom was slightly nervous about this, and he would mutter the words of the Initiation distractedly to himself when he thought that no one was listening. The fact that he had never had the chance to practice this piece of Magic before scared him more than he would admit to his twin sister and her best friend.

The trio made good progress that day. By evening, the young friends were about thirty miles south of Frenchville. At this rate, the three travelers would either reach the house late Tuesday evening or early Wednesday morning. The plan was for them to meet the next CLAIMED on Wednesday.

Tuesday went as planned. The young travelers stayed on Grace's schedule impeccably. The only trouble that they encountered was an over-crowded restaurant at noon, which led to a longer lunch stop than planned. Nonetheless, the children arrived in Frenchville late that evening and immediately tumbled into bed. It had been a long day.

Grace studied the map of Frenchville for a long time on Wednesday morning. She had trouble puzzling out where exactly the next CLAIMED lived. Eventually, with the twins' help, she figured out what the map meant and the children were on their way.

The young travelers strode rapidly down the two-lane streets and avenues of Frenchville. They turned on to a street called Ellis Lane and from there on to Robertson Way. The roads were old and gray, but many of them captivated Grace's imagination with their intriguing names.

Grace paused when she reached Robertson Way. She looked around at her surroundings and then studied the map that she had tightly clasped in her two hands. "This is it," she announced to Tom and Andrea. "This is the place where we need to be." She glanced at her friends to see if they had any comments.

"What number is the house again?" queried Andrea with a quizzical tilt to her head.

"15780 Robertson Way, Frenchville, Maine," Grace responded, grinning. "I've read that address so many times in the past week that I could recite it in my sleep."

Andrea nodded. "Right."

Grace nodded back. "That's what I said."

"No, that's not what I mean," cried Andrea, exasperated. "I meant it's on the right side of the road. See? The odd numbers are on the left, and the even numbers are to the right," Andrea explained.

"Oh. Sorry. I see now," Grace mumbled.

It took the trio a while for them to get to 15780. They stepped slowly, studying the mailboxes as they passed. Since 13298 had been the first box that they had seen, they had to march a long way before they spotted 15780.

"Look! There it is!" Tom called suddenly, pointing.

There it was. Grace didn't know what she had been expecting, but it certainly wasn't this. A great, brown structure made entirely of wood towered high above the other homes in the neighborhood. The three children stood quietly in awe. The sparkling windows were immaculate, and the great shutters on either side of the windows were free of grime and cobwebs. The porch that stuck out in front of the house was beautifully decorated. A large swing hung from the roof. Many colorful, bright pillows were piled on top of the swing. There were also two new wooden rocking chairs that rocked back and forth in the breeze.

Behind the house sat a small abandoned shed. It did not resemble the great house in the least. Vines grew untrimmed upon all the outer walls, and the walls themselves appeared rotten. The roof was sagging. It looked so unstable that Grace thought it was about to cave in. The white paint that had once covered the little building desperately needed to be redone. The grass, which was neatly trimmed everywhere else in the yard, grew high around the small structure as if to engulf it.

The children stood in the street, paused in indecision. The tall, lovely house was obviously the building in which the family resided, but something pulled Grace's eyes to the shed that lay in shambles behind the main building. For some reason, Grace was suddenly convinced that the person they were searching for was not a foster child, but instead a runaway who dreaded being found. Without any word to the others, she turned and began to head around to the back of the yard.

"Where are we going?" asked Andrea warily, afraid of being accused of trespassing. "We passed the door, Grace. It was around front."

"We're not going to the house," Grace responded, without glancing back. "We're going to the shed. Something tells me that the next of our new friends has not been as fortunate as Zachariah was."

Andrea and Tom did not question Grace's judgment. Her guesses had led them well so far; they had no reason to stop trusting her now.

The shed was in even worse condition close up. Some of the wood had already rotted away, leaving gaping holes in the walls. When the wind blew, it rocked the little structure on its foundation, causing it to creak as it swayed. Afraid for the shed's durability, Grace redirected the wind. It would not help their cause if the violent gusts of wind blew the shed down.

The children approached the door. The hinges had been permanently rusted in place, so the children did not even attempt to open it. They walked around the building, searching for a way to gain entry. Presently, they discovered

123

a hole in the back of the shed which was large enough for a person to crawl through.

The twins looked at Grace. "You're the leader; you go first."

Grace shook her head. "I don't want to go in there. It's dark and probably very dirty, too. You go first, Tom."

He shook his head. "Ladies first. It was your idea, anyway. And if you don't, I'm going up to the front door of that house and knocking and hoping the CLAIMED answers, if you don't have any better ideas. So are you going in or not?"

Grace frowned. She regarded the gaping hole with some trepidation. Finally, she got down on her hands and knees and crawled through the opening.

The inside of the building was not as dark as Grace had expected, because sunlight streamed in through the many holes, of which the entryway was only one. It was also not as dirty as expected, for someone had obviously been in there recently.

So her guess had some truth to it. For the most part, the shed was empty, but a small card table had been pushed against one of the walls. On it lay the remains of a poor meal—an empty chip bag, a banana peel, and a half-empty bottle of water. The peel looked fresh, and Grace wondered when the banana itself had been eaten.

Because, of course, no one was there.

Andrea cleared her throat from behind Grace. "Were we supposed to find someone here? 'Cause they're obviously gone now."

Grace sighed and turned around. "I'm sorry. Whoever it was must have left recently. I just thought—it seemed more likely—"

Something rustled in the leaves outside the opening. Or, rather, someone. A shadow fell through the hole, and Andrea glanced at Grace, her eyes darting like the eyes of a trapped rabbit. Grace shrugged as if saying, "I don't know. Don't ask me."

"What are you doing in my shed?" A hostile girl's voice cried.

Grace's head snapped away from Andrea, her eyes travelling to the opening. Crawling through the hole was a tall, tan, frighteningly thin girl. Her strait blonde hair had once been cut in a bob, but was now growing down to her shoulders. She spoke with an air that confirmed that she had been on the run for a while and was gaining confidence. She wore a tie-dyed tee-shirt that displayed faded colors, navy Bermuda shorts that had turned a dull gray, and a pair of cheap white tennis shoes that had unraveling laces. She wore no jewelry, but strapped to her back was a plain, no-nonsense black backpack. Grace guessed that it contained all of her belongings, despite its small size. *This girl probably doesn't own much, anyway,* she reasoned.

The girl stood and put her hands on her hips. "Well?" Her eyes were calm, but the rest of her face displayed hostility.

Grace stepped forward, her eyes just as calm as the strange girl's. "Hi, I'm Grace Foster. These are my friends, Andrea and Tom."

125

The girl did not budge. "You have not answered my question," she stated brusquely. "What are you doing in my shed?"

Grace took a deep breath and restarted. "Well, you see, we're orphans, too," she began.

"You don't look like it, act like it, or speak like it," the strange girl announced decidedly.

Grace huffed. This was not the way she wanted the conversation to go. This strange girl behaved with more hostility than Zachariah had, that was for sure. She had obviously run into some trouble before. "We *are* orphans," Grace continued. "But we have been more fortunate than most."

The strange girl looked affronted. "I'm not looking for charity, so you can take your good fortune back with you to wherever you came from," she responded. She was on the verge of just telling them to leave, but she knew that she must behave at least slightly civilly, or else she would give these unwanted strangers an advantage over her. At least, that's what she wanted them to believe she was doing. She was really just acting, but she hoped that the observant girl with the sandy blonde hair would not notice that.

"No, we will not leave," Grace replied firmly.

The girl was surprised. No one else who had come handing out charity had put up with such abrupt rudeness. "If you aren't handing out charity, then you must want something. What is it? I haven't got much."

Grace decided to be absolutely truthful. "We want you to come with us."

Grace had expected this to make the girl even more wary. On the contrary, the girl smiled broadly. "A strait answer, for once. Sit down, if you like. It isn't very comfortable, but"—she shrugged—"it's what I have."

Grace sat, wondering what had caused such a dramatic change in the girl's behavior. She stayed quiet, and hoped that neither she nor the twins would do something to make the strange girl go back to her harsh and unfriendly demeanor.

The girl plopped down on the ground and crossed her legs like a pretzel. "I used to have travelling buddies before," she explained. "But some policemen found them, and they were obviously suspicious of three poorly dressed teenagers who were alone. When the police found out who my friends were, they were taken right back to the orphanage as quickly as I could blink. I escaped capture and have been on my own ever since."

"If the ladies at the orphanage were actually nice, then why did you and your friends run away?" queried Tom suspiciously.

The girl frowned at him. "I thought you said you were orphans. Surely if you have been in an orphanage yourself, you would understand how it is?" Her tone sounded amazed but lacked anger.

Tom and Andrea shot each other loaded looks, but the girl failed to notice. Grace rapidly responded, "I'm sure you were bored. I remember some days in the orphanage..." She trailed off, shuddering in discomfort at the recollection.

The girl nodded. "We *were* bored. Cooped up in the same four walls, day after day, we longed for adventure. At first we planned on going back after a week or so, but we quickly realized that life on the road was more appealing."

Grace gave the girl a little half-smile. "I don't believe you told us your name," she whispered.

The girl grinned. "Right. I'm Dawn. Dawn Elizabeth Ellington, if you want to be precise. But typically people don't want to be precise." She shrugged. "Amazes me every day."

Grace laughed out loud. "Good to meet you, Dawn." She shook Dawn's hand, Andrea and Tom following after her. Tom frowned in concentration but smiled with relief when Dawn's eyes flashed a brilliant green.

Dawn frowned and shook her head. She knew that something had happened, but she didn't know what. She brushed it to the back of her mind and pasted another smile on her face. "Well, I've told you my story. Now, you tell me yours." She looked between the teenagers, and her eyes landed on Grace. Grace seemed to be the spokesperson.

Grace hesitated. "It's kind of hard to believe. In fact, it's absolutely ridiculous."

Dawn laughed. "I'm used to ridiculous."

"Alright," Grace began, still reluctant but knowing it was necessary. "Do you believe in Magic?"

Dawn did not act shocked or scared, nor did she look for a way around the situation, which surprised Grace, given the circumstances. Instead, she shrugged. "I've never really thought about it before. I mean, I guess I do."

Grace blinked. "What?"

"I said yes, I do," Dawn repeated, knowing her announcement had been shocking and grinning because of it.

"Oh," Grace responded faintly. "That's a first. Well, the thing is, me and my friends are Magicians. You have the power to be a great Magician, too, and you can come with us and learn how to use that power."

Despite Dawn's initial hostility, she was now more into the idea than either Grace or Zachariah had been. "Come with you to where?"

"To our Magic School. Our teacher is an orphan Magician, too." Grace caught the funny looks that Andrea and Tom were sending her and she realized that they hadn't known that. She blushed at the realization and stopped speaking.

"I'll come," Dawn announced. "I'm ready for a new adventure, and this will be a grand one, of that I'm sure."

Tom and Andrea beamed. Tom began, "Here's the plan: Dawn and I will be transported to you know where while we're still *here*." He gestured at their surroundings. "We'll travel on foot from there." The two girls nodded in understanding. They knew this meant, "We'll switch Dimensions while we're still in the shed and travel on foot through the Magic Dimension."

Grace and Andrea nodded, but Andrea smiled grimly. "I love you, brother," she whispered.

Tom nodded, his face as grim as his sister's. He grabbed Dawn's hand and began to murmur. The two teenagers popped out of sight.

16. The Right Road is Wrong

Andrea and Grace looked at each other for a few seconds before Andrea spoke, her voice coming out in a dry sob. "It's just the two of us now."

Grace nodded. "We should go back to the house we're staying at. We have no reason to be here anymore."

Andrea sighed and followed Grace as they crawled through the opening and back into the yard of the magnificent house. They hiked down the road in silence that was only occasionally interrupted by one of the girls sneezing or a bird chirping. Andrea wondered if Tom would prove to be a good leader as he travelled through an unknown part of the Magic Dimension. Grace knew that she was one step closer to being left alone in this Dimension, which unnerved her. She would soon have no help in figuring out maps, nor would she have a friend to talk to. *At least we have done well in our mission so far,* she thought. *We only have to get two more CLAIMED, and then our mission will be complete and we will finally be able to go home.* She sighed in pleasure just thinking about it.

Wrapped up as she was in her thoughts, Grace stumbled and bumped into Andrea. Andrea steadied her friend and they continued on in silence.

The house they were staying in while they were in Frenchville was relatively large, although not as enormous as the one in Hartford had been. It contained four bedrooms, but Andrea and Grace felt its emptiness keenly, so they slept on a bunkbed in the largest bedroom, which, surprisingly, was not the master bedroom. The house had nice furniture and the pantry had been well stocked, so the two children were quite comfortable.

Thursday arrived. The window in the girls' bedroom faced to the east, and they awoke to a brilliant sunrise. It was colored with oranges, yellows, pinks and blues that radiated out around the sun like an elaborate painting.

Grace leapt out of bed with a yawn. The sun's happy greeting cheered her and she grinned despite herself as a sudden feeling of joy and optimism exploded inside her. She landed lightly on the balls of her feet and bounced once before running back to stand beside the bed.

"Wake up, Andrea," she commanded, smiling. She shook her friend by the shoulders, urging her to awaken.

Andrea peered out from under the covers and laughed. "You look happy this morning," she announced, by way of greeting.

"It's one of those mornings that makes you forget all your worries and just want to laugh and sing for joy," she responded exuberantly. "Get up, sleepyhead, and look out the window. It's a beautiful day!"

Andrea climbed slowly out of bed and yawned. She stared out the window with appreciation. "Oh, wow," she breathed.

The girls ate breakfast and readied themselves for the day. Grace and Andrea examined the map carefully. Their next stop would be in Lebanon, New Hampshire, where the next of the CLAIMED lived.

The road was difficult to travel that day. In the morning, the hills caused the girls to have to hike

131

constantly. By noon, the exhausted teenagers had collapsed on a bench under a tree where they could rest and eat. They each wearily pulled a sandwich out of their bags. (They had packed lunch before they left that morning.) They quickly consumed the food but sat still for several minutes before continuing the hike.

The hills pestered the girls all through the afternoon and into the evening. To make things worse, the temperature climbed rapidly during the afternoon, and the blistering heat forced the children to travel under the trees instead of on the open pavement.

House number fifty-seven (the place where they rested that night) was small but air-conditioned. The two tiny bedrooms had been located close together, just down the hall from the living room. The tired girls fell into the soft beds with gratitude and slept dreamlessly until the morning.

It was Friday. Andrea and Grace left the house early in the morning, travelled over rough terrain, and collapsed into bed at night. That morning, they had woken up very sore from the tedious hike, but they were growing stronger with every passing day. Such became their daily routine: wake early, hike until late, and fall into bed with exhaustion at night.

Monday came and went. It had been three weeks. Twenty-one days. Grace would eventually stop counting, but right now it was a habit. She wondered how long it would be until she saw the Master again, or heard Jerra's voice, or studied at the School. She hoped it would not be long. She missed the School terribly. Most of all, she missed the Master, who had become like a mother to her.

Friday came again. The girls were nearing the New Hampshire-Maine border. By now, they had grown accustomed to the hills and rough roads, and their muscles no longer ached from the tedious hiking. Nevertheless, they continued to travel under the trees on account of the relentless sun.

Grace turned down the path, staying on the right side of the road as it forked. The girls continued walking, even as the road took them in a northwest direction.

It became late afternoon before Grace looked around and then stared at the map. The more she studied the paper and then looked around at their surroundings, the more sure she became. Finally, she placed a restraining hand on Andrea's shoulder to prevent her from walking any further. "Andrea," she whispered fearfully. "We're lost."

Andrea's eyes met Grace's own, and Grace could see her own fright reflected in her friend's gaze. "Where did we go wrong?" she whispered back, her face clouded with worry.

Grace frowned and replayed the day in her mind. She recalled the fork in the road, and her eyebrows shot up in remembrance. She studied the map, and it confirmed her suspicion. "I think we took the wrong turn at that split in the road," she answered.

"How long ago was that?" asked Andrea.

Grace shook her head. "Right before lunch. It was five *hours* ago…" She put her head in her hands and bit her lip, trying not to panic.

"So we've lost five hours. We just have to head back," stated Andrea calmly.

Grace nodded, wringing her hands in despair. "I'm so sorry, I—"

"Stop apologizing. It wasn't your fault. And even if it was, you shouldn't fret about it—you can't undo it now. I don't blame you; you were hot and tired and you made a simple mistake that anyone could have made. We just— need to go back before it gets too dark."

With another short nod, Grace turned and followed Andrea as she began to retrace their steps.

***

Grace gave a sigh and leaned against a tree. "It's no use, Andrea," she panted, wiping her hand against her forehead and staring in dismay at her empty water bottle.

They had been hiking back for only an hour and a half, but it was 5:45, and the sun had begun to set. The discouraged girls slumped against the trees while they caught their breath after the rapid travel.

"We'll never make it to the next house before dark, especially at this rate," Grace continued. "We're still four and a half *hours* away!" She made a face. "And we have been *running!* There's just no way."

Andrea frowned. She hadn't considered the fact that the sun was rapidly disappearing behind the trees. "You're right," she replied despondently. She studied Grace, her face calm but her eyes frantic. "What do you suggest that we do?

We obviously can't continue this—you've said that already."

Grace glanced at the area around them. As usual, they had been travelling in the trees, but the road lay not far from where they stood. They would be able to make rapid progress on the road while the sun was down and the darkness cooled the pavement. On the other hand, she knew that both of them needed to rest, whether or not they were near a house. They could not travel far tomorrow without sufficient sleep tonight. Grace scanned the trees, searching for a means of erecting a quick shelter.

An abundance of limbs and a few discarded boards were littered all over the forest floor. *It won't be a very stable shelter,* she realized, *but unless it rains it should be enough. And, of course, Andrea could help with that. Although—I seriously doubt she could redirect an entire rainstorm.*

Grace turned to Andrea. "We'll build a lean-to," she announced.

Andrea nodded. "Good idea."

Grace continued, "Collect as many boards as you can find. They'll work better than sticks, but if there aren't enough of them, we'll make do with some branches to fill in all the gaps."

Andrea moved quickly to follow Grace's orders. Grace, too, began to gather wood, scooping it up regardless of the many scratches it inflicted upon her arms. She was not one to sit around and wait while others worked to obey her commands.

135

When they had gathered enough material, the girls began to lean it against the largest tree that stood proudly near them. They constructed the shelter in the shape of a half-circle around the tree. Grace had found an old, abandoned tarp lying out near the road. It was slightly damp, but it would help keep out the dew. At first Grace thought it would prove to be too large, but then the girls discovered that they could fold it back so that it covered the ground underneath them as well as the leaning wall. The girls crawled inside the structure with their packs.

The room inside was rather cramped, hardly comfortable at all, but it beat sleeping out in the open woods by far. The loose tarp hung over the entrances, making a flap door on either end of the lean-to and blocking out the rapidly darkening woods. The girls huddled silently inside and curled up into two little balls, trying to keep themselves warm now that the night had descended.

The hours passed by slowly, marked by the distant tolling of a church bell. Try as they might, the girls could not fall asleep. They laid in too cramped of a position, and they cringed each time an owl hooted. They tensed at every noise, even the sound of a car whizzing past in the night. Finally, as the bell let out twelve rolling peals that signaled midnight's arrival, Grace rolled over and sighed.

Andrea let out a sigh, too. "Are you awake, Grace?"

Grace blinked. "More so than I wish to be, but yes."

"When are we leaving? We won't have to tidy up the house we've been staying in or make sure to lock the doors, at least. That's the good thing about spending the night in the woods."

"We'll get out of here around six-thirty. I doubt we'll be able to sleep at all, so we shouldn't have a problem there. After we eat a quick breakfast, we'll get on the road—probably around seven. We'll reach the next house around ten-thirty or eleven—" Grace jumped as something rustled the leaves outside of their tiny lean-to. Then she heard the whooshing of powerful wings and a loud hoot. She smiled. *It's just an owl.*

Andrea looked back at Grace, her face white in her fright. "Okay. So, I'm assuming we'll stay there until Monday—you know we'll have to rest after *this*." She gestured at their surroundings.

Grace gave a resigned sigh. "I know. We're so close to Lebanon I can almost taste it—and yet we're so far. I can't wait to meet the next CLAIMED, but..." she broke off and shrugged. "You're right."

Andrea sensed another reason for Grace's readiness to slow down and take a break. She gently rested a comforting hand on Grace's arm. "You are trying to stall. You don't want to be by yourself, is that it?" she questioned.

Grace nodded. "You know me too well." Her remark was followed by a small smile, but Andrea did not see it because the darkness concealed it from her view. Grace tried to relax on the hard ground, but it was no use. The dirt seemed determined to make her suffer.

Silence closed in around the girls once more. The chiming of the bells slowly repeated itself, but it was so far apart from the last chiming that it merely seemed to drag on the dreary silence.

The young girls were eventually consumed by the silence, and they fell unwittingly into an exhausted slumber.

***

Grace awoke. She still felt tired, but she resisted the urge to lay there and go back to sleep. She slowly forced her eyes to open. For a moment, she wondered where she was, but then it all came back to her—the mistake, the delay, and the miserable night in the woods. She slowly sat up, or at least, she sat up as far as the lean-to would allow.

Grace groaned audibly, and Andrea slowly blinked awake beside her. "What time is it?" Andrea croaked, her voice tired after the long and treacherous night.

Grace shook her head. "I have no idea." She felt hunger gnawing at her stomach, so she pushed the flap open.

Bright light poured into the lean-to from the woods, brighter than normal for early morning. The sunlight streamed through the trees, playing against the shiny leaves. The ground was wet with dew.

Andrea frowned. "Something tells me that it's later than we planned to leave," she remarked.

Suddenly the church bells rang out. The girls counted the chimes, which confirmed Andrea's hunch.

"Nine!" cried Grace. "Oh, my."

Grace let the tent flap fall back down. Andrea dug into their packs and removed two packets. "We can't leave without eating," she announced practically.

Grace grabbed her packet from Andrea and ate quickly, eager to get back on the road. This they accomplished, although not as soon as Grace had originally hoped. It was almost ten o' clock before they began to travel towards Lebanon once more.

The young girls were thankful for the nice weather that continued all through the day. The temperature felt warm even in the shade, but at least it was not rainy or night time. They travelled slowly, not running like they had the day before.

After roughly three and a half hours of hiking, the girls came back to the split in the road, the place that had caused them so much trouble. They studied the roads carefully and selected the correct path. Grace sighed, grateful that they were headed in the right direction once more. They were headed in the direction in which the next CLAIMED lay.

The woods were now tangled with briars and much overgrowth, which, a few days ago, would have greatly discouraged the girls. Now, though, they simply redirected their path on to the open pavement to avoid the hampering conditions. It seemed such a small misfortune, compared to what they had endured yesterday.

It took an hour of travelling after the fork in the road for the girls to reach the next house, house number twenty-four. The tired girls collapsed in the soft beds, weary of walking, talking, and planning. It did not take long for both of the girls to fall into a deep slumber.

17. The Unexpected Journey

Grace felt herself drifting off to sleep. The next thing she knew, she was jostled awake as the cart went over bump.

Wait—the cart? She blinked, confused, as she tried and failed to identify her surroundings.

She had been thrown in the back of a horse-drawn carriage. Apparently, she had not been restrained, for which she was grateful. The people who were driving the cart must not have thought that she was much of a threat. She felt slightly cross at this (after all, she was the second most powerful Magician ever, and the most powerful Magician who was currently living). However, her thankfulness over not being bound soon enveloped her annoyance at being disregarded as weak.

A gruff voice in the front seat suddenly barked, "Turn right, son. After we go a mile, we'll be in New Yorin state again. We'll take our new little friend to Kamryn's place." Grace heard someone else inhale sharply in annoyance. "Kamryn will take care of her," the man with the gruff voice continued.

Grace felt her muscles tense in alarm as she sat up. One of the three people in the front seat turned around with a smile. Grace instantly noticed his graying hair, wrinkled skin, and dirty clothes. He was the man with the gruff voice. "Hello, little 'un. What happened to you? You were knocked out cold when we found you, and the house behind you was smoldering. Some nasty criminal's work, I'll bet."

Grace felt as if someone else was shaking her head for her. Her voice came as though through water, even though she had not willed herself to speak. "Oh, no, it wasn't a criminal. That was my doing. Even *you* should have been able to see that." She lifted her chin haughtily. Grace frowned, shocked that her tongue had moved on its own, and that it spoke such lies. Her head had moved as if it was making its own decisions, without her consent.

The man in the front seat failed to notice her mental confusion. He laughed at her words. "You?" he asked in utter disbelief. "Why would you do such a thing?" His face was perfectly serious, but his eyes laughed silently at her.

Grace's shoulders shrugged without her consent. "It was an accident," she replied simply. "I didn't mean to do it—it just kind of—happened."

The man stared at her. "That—" he waved his hand vaguely back the way they had come. "—you say that was an accident?"

"It was!" Grace's tongue cried hotly. "I didn't *mean* to do it, honest."

"Well, then," the man replied, trying to calm her. "I'm sure you didn't mean to do it. But how did it happen?"

Grace's lips smiled mischievously. "I was having a bad day. I was mad. I tend to cast Spells unintentionally when I'm so furious. Well—I kind of blew up the house with a fireball. It wasn't the fireball itself that knocked me out, though—it was me using too much of my Magic at once."

All three men turned to stare at her. "Using that much Magic at once would have *killed* an ordinary person!"

141

they exclaimed in disbelief. "There's no way you could have—how in the world did you do it?"

The girl stated calmly, "I'm in the Magic sector Enchanted. I'm a powerful Magician."

The first man nodded. "That tends to explain a lot of things—the least of which being how you managed to destroy your house."

The group fell silent. Grace sat uncomfortably in the back of the cart, wondering when and what her mouth would choose to say next. Today it seemed like her body parts all had minds of their own.

The shortest man, who was wearing an emerald-green suit and reminded Grace of a character in a book she had once read, spoke up. "We're back in New Yorin. Jolly good to be home—if not for a few little details." The short man glared at the driver. "I never thought we'd be coming back with a little 'un in tow, though."

"I'm not that little," Grace's tongue announced. Her eyes glared at the short man. "I'll be seven next week."

Grace almost boiled over in frustration. What was wrong with her? Why was her body not cooperating—even lying? Couldn't the man see she wasn't seven? He was not unreasonable, Grace knew.

Obviously he could not tell that she was older than seven. He chuckled at her response. "True."

The wagon continued down the street. Occasionally, Grace got knocked around when it went over a bump or around a curve. The horse plodded on at a steady pace. Grace wondered if it was just really well-trained or if it could go on forever without tiring. Grace let out a sigh of exasperation as she rolled over against her will. *I must be under a Spell*, she concluded. *But why? And who put me under such a powerful Spell?*

Her thoughts evaporated as her tongue began to speak. "What are you going to do with me?"

The man in the emerald suit laughed. *He thinks everything is funny*, noticed Grace resentfully. The man answered carefully, glancing at the driver as her spoke. "We have a—" he searched for the right word "—friend. She is strong in Magic and very kind. She will take you in."

Grace's instant relief was swept away as her tongue replied, "You don't want me?" Her tone was that of immense disappointment.

The man shook his head, but he grinned. "No. What use would we have for a little one? You would only get in the way."

Grace's head nodded reasonably. Suddenly a thought struck her with enough force that it would have knocked her over—if she had been in control of her body. *Where's Andrea?!?* She tried to cry out, but her tongue lay in her mouth as still and as heavy as lead.

"Here we are," the man who was driving announced. His voice sounded strained, but it was also filled with longing.

Grace failed to notice, though. Her head shot up and peered over the edge of the wagon in curiosity. Before her lay a vast field. She had been jostled around a good deal for the most recent part of the journey, and now she could see why. They had long since left the road, and now they were

143

travelling through a vast expanse of grass. Only one solitary building protruded out of the smooth meadow.

It was a small house. The house sat, one story high, completely surrounded by all of that grass. It was a brick house, but it had been painted white. The neat black shingles that covered the roof reflected the sunlight like glitter.

The wagon began to move again, heading towards the lonely building. It bounced along in the grass, which made Grace highly uncomfortable. Her head hit the side of the wagon, and she winced in pain.

The group soon arrived in front of the little cottage. The man who had, until that point, been driving the cart, now leapt down and hurried towards the black door at the front of the house.

A short woman with red cheeks, black hair, and a kind face opened the door. "Who are you?" she queried, her expression guarded.

The man looked hurt. "Do you not recognize me, Kamryn?" the man asked, his voice soft.

"I…" The woman looked puzzled and shook her head. Then her eyes widened in hope, and Grace could see tears in them. "Jacob?" she whispered. He nodded. The woman flung her arms around him.

"Kamryn," Jacob replied, and Grace could hear the smile in his voice. "I missed you, as well." His voice was gentle and tender. "Look, Kam. I brought Timothy and Father today, too." The man in the emerald suit scowled. "Oh, and on our way, we found this child. She had fainted— we thought you might be able to help her."

Kamryn looked away from Jacob, towards the wagon. Grace may have imagined it, but she thought that she saw Kamryn's expression harden into dislike at the sight of the man in the emerald suit. Her face melted into compassion, though, when she noticed Grace. "Come along, all of you, come in. You are welcome at my house. I'll fix some tea and a snack for all of us," she announced with a smile.

The elderly man headed for the house, but the man in the emerald suit—presumably Timothy—picked Grace up out of the back of the wagon and swung her down on to the ground. "Come, child," he directed, his voice merry but his eyes cautious. "I can see time has not hurt Kamryn and Jacob, although it has been three years. I was a fool to think it might have. I should not have brought you here." He strolled slowly, absorbed in his thoughts. He seemed reluctant to follow the others into the house. "I wonder at them, though. How could Jacob do this to me, when I so need him? It is quite frustrating, honestly." He turned the doorknob and followed Grace in.

Grace felt surprised that the door had not opened itself. However, she did not speak of it, seeing as her body was acting as though it had a mind of its own. *Perhaps,* Grace thought wearily, *it* does *have its own mind.*

Timothy left the main room as quickly as possible, mumbling that he was tired. He entered one of the six rooms that lined the main living room. Grace supposed that the door must lead to a bedroom.

The elderly man fell asleep on the couch almost instantly. Jacob sat down next to Kamryn on the other

145

couch, gazing about the room in silence. Grace seated herself in the only remaining place—a chair situated in the darkest corner of the room.

"Where's Violet?" queried Jacob. "Is she okay?"

"Relax," Kamryn mumbled, leaning back against the couch. "She's fine. She's just asleep—after all, she's only four."

Jacob put his head in his hands. "She won't remember me, though. She was only one... Oh, Kamryn, I'm so sorry."

"I..." Kamryn shook her head. "I've told her of you countless times, you know—she loves to hear of her father."

Grace gasped, unable to keep silent any longer. *"What?"*

Jacob turned around, a pleasant smile on his lips. "I forgot you were here. Kamryn, this is the girl I told you about. Her name is..." He looked at Grace for help.

"Rose. My name is Rose," Grace's mouth completed.

"Rose," continued Jacob, "this is my wife, Kamryn Matthews."

Kamryn smiled, but it did not reach her eyes. "Jacob's brother is very—how shall I put this—bossy. He needed Jacob's help to do something, and he needed to do it far away. He was very inconsiderate of me and Violet. But, yes, Jacob went." She glanced at her husband, hurt in her eyes.

Jacob bowed his head sadly. "I had to help—you know what he was doing, Kamryn! We both knew I would be back soon—his mission was only temporary."

"It was *three years*, Jacob!" Her eyes were sad. "Are you going to leave again when he goes? I am sure he will be starting another project soon."

"No! Oh, no, Kamryn, I could never. I am not going to go back with him. He's just going to have to learn to do—whatever he's doing—by himself."

Kamryn embraced him. "Oh, Jacob." Grace could see the tears rolling down her cheeks. "I missed you, and Violet..." she trailed off.

From somewhere else, Grace could hear a distant voice. "Grace! Gracine Foster! Wake up!"

18. Onward Travel

Grace opened her eyes and sat up. She was in house number twenty-four, and Andrea stood over her.

"I…" Grace mumbled, looking around. "I just…"

"Good morning, sleepyhead," greeted Andrea. "It's Sunday. And it's *ten o' clock!* Plus, it took me at least a minute to wake you."

Grace glanced around sleepily, relieved to see that she was back at house number twenty-four and that she had regained control of her body. "I was tired, so I slept like a rock." She gave Andrea no indication of her vivid dream. "I could have slept a good while longer if you hadn't awakened me."

Andrea shook her friend sharply by the shoulders. "I'll say you slept like a rock. I've never in all my life seen anyone who slept that hard—not even Tom." Her eyes flickered with amusement. "And he sleeps the hardest of all of the people I know—after you, of course."

"Ha, ha. Very funny." Grace rolled her eyes. "Honestly, Andrea—even I don't sleep as hard as your brother—he's impossible." She chuckled as she climbed out of bed and stretched. "Although, I do admit—I wish I could sleep that hard sometimes." She began to make up the bed, but Andrea waved her off.

"You came pretty close to your wish last night," she remarked. "But never mind making the bed." Andrea spoke a simple Charm, and the bed rapidly made itself.

Grace frowned at her. "That was hardly necessary. You know we aren't supposed to do Magic unless absolutely no other option is presented—and I'd say you had a choice right now, wouldn't you?"

Andrea crossed her arms, teasing Grace's strict rule-following. "A simple 'thank you' would suffice."

Grace glanced at her friend and smiled wryly. "Thank you, Andrea. I appreciate you making my bed for me, even if it is not *technically* allowed."

Andrea bowed comically. "My pleasure. Now, come to breakfast. I've been waiting on you for so long, I'm starved!"

"When did you get up?" Grace queried.

Andrea glanced at her. "Six hours ago. Four o' clock, to be precise. You are kind of a long sleeper. At first I was just going to wait until you got up, but you insisted on sleeping until next year, so I was forced to awaken you. Even then..." She shook her head in amazement.

"You got up at *four?!?* I guess you might be a little hungry, then." Grace laughed.

Andrea shrugged. "I got used to my rumbling stomach after a while. Come *on,* let's go eat! Do you want me to faint?"

The girls laughed as they entered the kitchen. They each grabbed a packet and together they devoured their breakfast.

That was a lovely day. The girls stayed at the house and rested, and Grace thought no more on her strange and confusing dream. The two girls played cards, read, and otherwise filled their time with small tasks that could never help their mission. Even though the girls knew that their activities were pointless as far as getting the CLAIMED was concerned, they still enjoyed the small games and other trivial activities.

The next night contained no dreams for Grace, frightening or otherwise. This gladdened her. No strange family quarrels or vicious wolves that attacked her home filled her head tonight, allowing her a complete rest.

Monday dawned. The sky contained a few white clouds, scattered across it like massive marshmallows. The beautiful blue of the sky itself spanned from horizon to horizon, and the rays of sunlight that came down through the clouds made brilliant sunbeams that shimmered down to earth and disappeared.

The girls continued to hike across the northern states. The day felt cool, much more pleasant for travel than the ones the girls had recently encountered. An occasional breeze teased Grace's dark ponytail into a mass of tangles, but she didn't mind. She could always brush them out later, and the day was ideal for hiking. The absence of the blistering heat allowed the girls to travel out in the open instead of under the trees. Grace hoped travelling on the road would help prevent mistakes such as the one they had made on Friday.

Sometime around the middle of the day, the girls crossed the New Hampshire-Maine border. The girls grinned at the signs. "Welcome to New Hampshire!" read plainly on all of them.

"We're so close!" gasped Grace. "I can almost taste it. Only a couple more days, now." She felt relieved that they would soon take care of the third CLAIMED, despite all the trouble that they had encountered trying to get to Lebanon.

She completely failed to notice that it was Monday. It was the four-week anniversary of the beginning of their mission.

Grace wondered what Tom and the others were doing at the moment. By now both Dawn and Zachariah would be well into their Magical studies. The Master was probably too busy to miss Andrea and Grace, or even to be concerned about how they were doing in their travels. Grace shuddered. *I need to stop thinking like that,* she reprimanded herself.

All the same, she still missed the Master—and Jerra, who had become like an older sister to her. Much to her surprise, she even missed—she laughed to think of it—*Tom!* Tom, who annoyed her and Andrea to no end, who held back, and didn't help on the mission. She snorted. She missed Tom!

Grace sighed and kicked a rock out of her path. She had firmly decided not to think about things such as those, but her mind kept lingering on the subject. It was so hard not to think on it. Still, she resolved to temporarily turn off her imagination. Instead, she planted her thoughts on the mission ahead.

If she and Andrea continued faithfully travelling at their current speed, then they should reach Lebanon by late tomorrow or early Wednesday. They would meet the next CLAIMED on Wednesday!

19. Michael

Grace and Andrea continued on, arriving in Lebanon late on Tuesday. The day of hiking had been long and tiring, due to the fact that they had left extra early that morning. The girls fell into bed and slept soundly.

Grace set the alarm clock in her room for seven in the morning. It beeped loudly, seeming to drill into her head with its shrill screams. She rolled over and turned it off. She clambered out of bed and quickly made the bed up by non-Magical means.

Andrea still slept, so Grace tiptoed down the hall, trying not to wake her friend. She walked slowly and carefully. They were in Lebanon! Her excitement was extreme. They would meet the next CLAIMED today! She stopped tip-toeing and bounced into the small, colorful, and cheerful kitchen.

Grace decided not to reach for a packet this morning. Instead, she hungrily devoured a bowl full of cereal topped with strawberries and blueberries. Someone had thoughtfully left the box of cereal on the table so that it would not be hard to locate. Grace mentally thanked whoever it was as she ate her breakfast.

Andrea entered the kitchen, appearing drowsy but not ill-tempered. "Good morning!" She greeted Grace with a smile as she sat down to her own bowl of cereal. The chair she pulled out from under the table squeaked against the floor, but it quieted as she sat down.

"Good morning," responded Grace. She removed a map from her pack and placed it on the table. "Here we are." She pointed to a spot marking a house on the map of Lebanon. "Where do you suppose the next CLAIMED is?" The map gave her no hints as to where a young orphan would live, especially if the aforesaid orphan did not want to be found.

Andrea shrugged. "N' clue," she mumbled through a mouthful of cereal. "I mean, I have no clue," she amended after she had swallowed.

Grace took out the map that Jerra had given her, the map detailing the locations of the four CLAIMED. She studied it for a few minutes. The town was of a good size, not so large that it would take days to find the next CLAIMED, but not so small that it was only a couple of buildings and one stoplight. Finally, she came to a conclusion and marked the spot on her map of Lebanon.

The girls finished breakfast and gathered up their things. Andrea and Grace spoke very little as they worked. Neither of them voiced the fact they both had printed in the forefront of their minds—Andrea would be leaving today, and Grace would be alone.

They left the house in the middle of the morning, heading west. The day was bright and sunny, and the temperature was starting to mount. While it had been cool in the early morning when the dew was fresh on the grass, the day was getting warmer, and soon it would verge on being hot. The girls traveled in the shade again so they could avoid the sun's intense glare, and they were thankful for an occasional breeze.

Soon Grace turned and headed towards the south. Then west again. Then, for a very short time, she turned and walked north.

They entered a one-way road overshadowed by large, old and beautiful buildings. Grace frowned and looked away from the buildings, but Andrea was enthralled. She studied the lovely walls and looked up towards the rooftops.

Grace, on the other hand, ignored the buildings. The beauty and art displayed in their architectural design failed to amaze her. She sat down on the curb, puzzled. She felt sure this was it—this was where they needed to be. But the street contained no houses, nor homes of any sort. Grace saw no building that looked like a suitable place to live— there were only office buildings and shops. Grace glanced around, befuddled. *Strange.*

Grace frowned and examined the street more closely. A few people were strolling down it, some on their own and others in pairs or trios. None of them took any notice of the two girls who stood uncertainly on the side of the road.

A young boy, who looked about fourteen, ran down the street. He was tall but not extremely so. Attached to his back was a big brown backpack that was stuffed to the point of overflowing, despite its size. The large bag did not hamper the boy's speed as he raced off down the street.

Grace hardly noticed him. She looked up and turned to Andrea. "Where should we go now?"

Andrea stared at the boy. "Nowhere. We're here. That's him."

Grace frowned at her. "What? How do you know?"

Andrea shrugged. "I just know. It's one of those things that just come with intuition. Now come *on*, we don't want to lose him!" Andrea began to run after the strange boy.

Grace thrust out her arm to stop her friend. "Andrea, wait. What are you intending to say? You can't just say, 'Hi, I'm a Magician, and you should come with me to my Magic School. Oh, and if you don't come, I'll turn you into a toad.' There's no *way* he'll believe you."

"The thing to do first," Andrea explained, beginning to get impatient. She glanced after the boy, who was getting further away. She spoke in a rush, "The thing to do first is to Initiate his Magic. That will make him curious, even without us saying anything suspicious."

Grace nodded. "You're right. But we can't let anyone else see the green eyes. Be careful and cautious in everything you do and say. Something tells me he'll be harder to catch than even Dawn."

By now the boy had run a good block further up the street. The girls began to pelt after him, but it was no use. He ran too fast for the two amateur sprinters to catch up with him. He bolted around a corner and out of sight.

The panting girls sat down on the curb. Grace hunched over in embarrassment. She had come so far, only to let the CLAIMED get away once they found him. She was a failure as a leader. A single tear rolled down her cheek.

The girls sat there for a good ten minutes, contemplating what to do next. They had found the next CLAIMED—but then they had lost him. *We just have to find him again,* Grace reasoned. *If we can slow him down enough to talk to him, then we should be okay.*

She glanced down the street in the direction that he had gone. She blinked, not sure that she was seeing correctly, but hoping that she was. She tapped Andrea and pointed down the road. "Look, he's coming back!" she cried in triumph.

It was true. Pelting down the street towards them at a remarkable speed was the strange boy.

Grace stood quickly. "Stop!" she yelled, not knowing any other way to make him understand that they wanted to talk to him before he passed them by completely. "Hey, you! Please stop!"

He slowed down. His black hair shined in the sun. His thin frame glistened with sweat, and he was unnaturally tan. *Probably from running around outside all the time,* Grace thought. His eyes were a brilliant blue. He approached them with an air that was wild yet cautious—his expression reminded Grace of a cornered animal, an animal that would either run away or attack at a moment's notice.

This is, of course, why she spoke to him quietly—she understood that he was wild in nature. "Hi," she greeted, facing the street so that he would have to face away from it. She reached out her hand to shake his.

The boy did not shake it, but instead looked at it as though it were absolutely repulsive. He looked at Andrea, his eyes wary.

"Hello," she repeated, extending her hand as well.

The boy frowned there was a deep calculating expression behind his eyes, and his guarded countenance did not soften. "Who are you?" he asked gruffly.

"Travelers," Grace replied, offering only a small portion of the truth. "Is there a good place we can stay around here?" she quickly continued.

The boy detected the lack of truth and picked her story apart at once. "Where did you stay last night?" he asked. "You look fully rested. Or did you arrive this morning? And where's your car? Did you not travel with an adult?"

Grace blinked. His instant and automatic counter-attack had muddled her.

Andrea stepped forward and lightly rested her hand on the boy's arm. "She's not lying. Leave her alone." In the instant that Andrea had her hand on his arm, the boy's eyes flashed green.

He stepped back and shook his head to clear it. "Go away, or I'm going to tell my father!" he yelled in surprise.

This was his greatest mistake. "You don't have a father," Grace responded, her voice quiet but poisonous. "Your father is dead—and he has been for over ten years."

The shock registered on the boy's face. "How did you know that?" he snapped, before he thought to deny it. He narrowed his eyes in suspicion. "You've never met me before. So how did you *know* that?!?"

Grace shrugged. "I know more than you think I do."

The boy nodded. He understood that she was telling the truth. "But *how*?" he whispered, afraid of this strange girl who knew so much about him, even though she had never seen him before.

Grace shrugged again. "That's my little secret."

The boy frowned and shook his head slightly as if to shake off a fly. "Who are you?" he asked again, but this time his tone did not contain as much hostility, only innocent curiosity and a little fear.

"I'm Grace." Grace extended her hand, and this time, the boy shook it.

"I'm Andrea." Andrea shook his hand as well. "Who might you be?"

"Michael," the boy responded in a dazed voice. "Michael West."

The trio stood there awkwardly for a moment, each person unsure of what to say next. Finally, Grace broke the ice with the startling yet vitally important question. "Do you believe in Magic?"

Much to the girls' surprise, he answered the question in a way much like Dawn had. He merely shrugged. "I don't know. I mean, I guess I do."

Grace stared at him before continuing. "What would you say if I told you that you are a Magician, and a very powerful one, too?"

Michael frowned. "Why would you say that?"

Grace looked at Andrea hesitantly. "It's a rather long story."

"Well, I believe you about the Magic and all that." Michael had lost all of his former caution and hostility.

"Look, though. We're from a Magic School," began Andrea. "You need to come with us back to the School, so you can learn to use Magic, too."

Michael nodded. "Let's go!"

Andrea grabbed his hand and smiled. "I'll see you, Grace." She began to whisper, and she, along with Michael, popped out of sight.

Grace was alone.

20. A New Destination

Grace blinked. Then a sudden realization swept over her—she was by herself. Now, she was truly alone. An emotion hit her in a wave—an emotion that she had been expecting least of all—joy.

She blinked again, surprised. She had been dreading this moment for a month. Now it was finally here—and she felt *happy?* Grace frowned. *I'm going crazy.* Still, she could not shake the optimistic feeling that bubbled up within her. She laughed aloud, her voice ringing off the tall buildings and causing some people to shoot her curious glances. She felt so *free!*

Grace pelted down the road as fast as she could go. Her feet flew along the pavement, as strong and as fast as the wings of a soaring eagle. At that moment, she felt like she could beat even Michael in a race.

By the time Grace reached the house, she was completely out of breath and panting like a dog. She sat down on a chair with a resounding *thump!*, breathing hard. She gulped down a glass of ice-cold water. The frigid drink felt cool and refreshing as it rushed down her dry throat. She leaned back and sucked contentedly on an ice-cube from the glass.

A drop of sweat rolled down Grace's forehead. She brushed it off and stood. She headed to take a shower. When she had finished, she ran down the hall, jumped as high as she could, and landed squarely in the middle of the bed. In a few minutes, she had fallen fast asleep. She did not wake until the next morning.

Thursday dawned. When Grace finally sat up in the bed, all of the unnatural enthusiasm from the night before was gone, leaving her feeling drained and tired. Nonetheless, she dragged herself out of bed and prepared for the long hike.

Grace looked up her next destination on the map, and her heart leaped with joy. Once she re-entered the Magic Dimension, she would not have far to go before she reached the School—for, much to Grace's delight, the next CLAIMED lived in New York City.

Grace knew instantly that this CLAIMED would be different from the foster child Zachariah, the runaway Dawn, and the homeless Michael. All of them had such unique stories, and Grace was sure that this new CLAIMED would be just as special. Grace was also sure, somehow, that this CLAIMED would be the most difficult of all to convince. *Oh, well*, she thought, *I'll convince the* CLAIMED *in some way*.

The road lay out smoothly before Grace, now that she was headed back south towards New York. The temperature felt unnaturally gentle—neither brutally hot nor frighteningly chilly. Grace set off, thankful, stepping quickly and confidently on her way.

The road encouraged her ever onward. Dark fell at five o' clock, yet Grace had not yet reached the next house. Rather than spending another night in the woods, Grace chose to continue onward, enjoying the exertion.

An hour passed before Grace finally reached the next house, which lay almost fifty miles south of Lebanon. She had traveled an amazing distance that day. It took her no time at all to fall asleep.

***

She sat once more in the living room at Kamryn Matthew's house. Across from her sat Timothy, whose countenance was covered with disbelief and ferocity. He was talking rapidly. The two of them were the only people in the room, for the time was long past midnight.

"It has been an entire *week*, Rose!" Timothy exclaimed. "A week since we arrived here. I was a fool to return here. I should have known he would choose not to come back with me. And now..." He put his head in his hands, suddenly appearing tired.

Grace's tongue moved, speaking with harsh finality. "Would you keep a man and his wife apart, not to mention their little child? You are a cruel man if that is what you wish to do, Timothy Matthews."

"No!" Timothy cried, indignation in his voice at being reproved by a seven-year-old. "I am not cruel, but I do believe that the well-being of the entire world is more important than the temporary happiness of one family!" He slammed his fist against the couch to punctuate his point.

"It is not your decision to make," Grace's tongue responded, boldly defending Jacob's choice. "Your brother is in charge of his life, even if it is not the life you want him to live."

"Jacob has helped me much these past few years," Timothy responded. "We have put many Enchantments in place to keep this country and the world protected from the Darkniss for many years to come. He has helped me with everything—and now, on the final Enchantment, he leaves. He gives up. He abandons his brother."

"He has a right," Grace's tongue reminded Timothy.

"He knows—he *knows*, mind you—that if I do this Enchantment by myself that I will almost certainly die. And yet—I must do the Enchantment. If I want to defeat the Darkniss—and I do—than I must."

Grace's head nodded. "It is as you say."

"You will stay here with Kamryn and Jacob, then," announced Timothy decidedly. "Farewell, Rose. I wish you well." With that, Timothy picked up his bag and walked out the front door, leaving, despite the fact that it was almost midnight. Or, perhaps, because it was almost midnight. "Say goodbye to the others for me," he whispered. He closed the door and was gone into the night.

***

Grace's eyes opened slowly. She surveyed her surroundings, glancing around the room that she was sleeping in. It was still dark; the moon still shone high in the sky. Except for the blanket that she had unknowingly kicked off the bed, the room was the same as it had been when she had gotten into bed.

163

She blinked, remembering the dream. It had been much shorter this time. But why had she awoken? Andrea was not shaking her. And why had it continued at all?

She thought back to her frightening dream about Jerra. Maybe this dream, like that one, was a real event from the past. In which case... it could have much more to do with Grace than she had previously believed. Grace shuddered, wondering what it could possibly have to do with her. What was it even about? And why was she dreaming it?

She rolled over, knowing that she could do nothing to test her theory at the moment. She would be forced to wait to ask the Master until she got back home, assuming that she even remembered to tell the Master about the dream in the first place.

Her thoughts drifted away from the dream, and soon she had once more fallen asleep, while thinking about going home.

21. The Last CLAIMED

The days passed quickly for Grace. She traveled faster now, working on her speed as well as her endurance.

By Wednesday, around noon, Grace had reached Gretchen's house outside of New York City.

Gretchen opened the door slowly. Her face lit up as she recognized Grace, and she smiled. "Come in, child, come in!" she cried joyously. "I've been wondering when I would see you again. I've been thinking about you these past five weeks, you know. Are you getting close to the end yet? I suppose you are, since the others are no longer with you."

Grace nodded as she entered the house. She lifted her nose and took in deep breaths of the delicious, fresh scent. "What are you making?" she asked. "It smells positively wonderful." She looked around, trying to locate the source of the smell.

"Oh, I'm making a cake. I had a feeling I would need it soon." She smiled down at the child. "But, dearie me, look at what I'm doing! You must be exhausted, child, please sit down. I'll get you something to eat."

Grace obeyed, glad to be with someone that she knew after a week of being alone. She sighed gratefully as she sank into a chair and devoured the warm food. "How do you manage to make such wonderful food?" she queried in amazement.

Gretchen shrugged, smiling. "It's a natural talent. I inherited it from my mother; she was always a wonderful cook."

Grace rested upstairs that afternoon. She did what she would typically call "purely wasting time." Today, though, she deemed it necessary. *It's good to have a break after travelling for so long*, she thought gratefully.

Before she knew, Thursday had arrived. She climbed out of bed, ate breakfast, and pin-pointed the location of the last CLAIMED. At ten o' clock in the morning, Grace hugged Gretchen goodbye and thanked her. Finally, she departed to find the last of the four new CLAIMED.

She had discovered that the CLAIMED lived not inside of New York City itself but outside of it, like Gretchen. How exactly this young person managed to live was a mystery to Grace. She felt positive that the person was neither fostered, nor runaway, nor homeless. But what this person was confounded Grace. How would the CLAIMED be living, since all of the CLAIMED were orphans?

It took Grace not even five minutes to reach a quaint little cottage with a long gravel driveway. The driveway, which curved back towards the house, was bordered with tall, graceful trees. As for the house itself, it was a small thing, surrounded by beds of flowers. A tiny front porch extended from the door, and it was attached to the driveway by a narrow sidewalk. A single oak tree towered over the house.

Grace took in a deep breath as she studied the little house. It appeared to be well-taken-care of, that was for sure; the bushes were neatly trimmed and the grass had

166

recently been cut. *Maybe I was wrong, after all*, Grace thought. *Maybe this child is actually a foster child. I wonder why I thought it was otherwise.*

Or maybe I'm at the wrong house. That would explain it. Grace considered the possibility. It could be true, she could be at the wrong house—but she decided that that was highly unlikely. Her Magic had never failed before— why would it fail her now? She checked the map again. *Yes—I'm at the right house.*

Grace frowned. *Should I just go up and knock? I hope someone's home. What a tangle I would be in if they weren't. I have to trust that they are, but...* She grimaced, standing in the middle of the road, paused in indecision.

She blinked. Yes, someone was definitely home, for the little door on the front of the house was slowly opening. Someone stuck their head out of the door, looking around with a searching expression.

A smile spread across Grace's face as she watched. The little girl, probably about twelve in age, gave a very sharp, very piercing whistle. Much to Grace's delight, a fiery red squirrel flew across the yard in giant leaps.

The squirrel quickly darted up the sidewalk and into the front door. The girl looked around. She did not notice Grace. The girl's head, which was covered in a mass of red curls, disappeared into the house as the door closed.

The grin slowly melted off of Grace's face. She felt sure that this girl with the pet squirrel was the last of the CLAIMED, but she still didn't know if the girl was alone or if there was someone else in the house. *There's no way to find out,* she thought miserably. I just have to hope that she opens the door and not someone else.

Grace finally gained the courage to cautiously approach the house. It felt strange for her to be scared of a little girl in a tiny house, but she was. Slowly and deliberately, she made her way up to the front door. She knocked sharply. "Hello?" she called. "Is anyone home?"

A girl's voice sounded faintly from behind the door. "No. Now go away. The person who lives here does not want people coming to her house when she is away."

Grace grinned. "Come out, please. I won't hurt you."

"You should be more concerned about whether or not I will hurt you," responded a highly annoyed voice. It was not an idle threat.

Grace frowned. "Come out," she coaxed. "I'm not afraid of you, nor will I hurt you—but I do want to talk to you."

"I'm sure the conversation will go as usual," proclaimed the girl sarcastically. "Something like this:" (here she imitated a high, sickly sweet lady's voice) "'So, dear, where did you say your parents were again?'" (she changed back to her normal voice) "'I told you; I don't have any parents—at least anymore. And *don't* call me dear!' And then whoever it is says, 'So this is where you live—is your aunt or uncle home?' To which I reply, as always, 'No, I live here alone. And alone I'd like to stay, so you are welcome to go away immediately!'" The girl took a deep breath.

Grace's frown deepened. The door still had not opened, and she was finding it hard to hear the girl. It also

168

frustrated her immensely to be having a conversation with someone who was on the other side of a door, especially if that someone had no intention of opening it. "Come outside, girl! I'm not going away, mind you. I will sit out here for hours, if necessary. Just come out, *please*."

The door opened a tiny bit. A freckled nose stuck out through the crack. "Fine," the girl mumbled.

Grace smiled. She felt a shimmer of encouragement. "Hello. I'm Grace Foster, and, in case you haven't already noticed, I'm not an adult."

The girl's entire face peered out from behind the door. From her expression, Grace judged that she felt rather foolish. "Oh. So I see."

"Now will you come out?" Grace asked urgently.

The girl sighed and rolled her eyes, as if Grace wasn't really worth her time. She reluctantly finished opening the door and stepped out. She scooped up the red squirrel as it was scampering out of the house. With great care, she set it on her shoulder. Finally, she turned to Grace and smiled grimly. "I suppose I should introduce myself as well." She rolled her eyes again. "I am Hazel Grant. Hazel *Whitney* Grant, to be specific."

Grace almost laughed. The way she had introduced herself was so similar to the way that Tom had introduced himself the day that Grace arrived at the School. The tone of voice differed, to be sure—Tom's voice had sounded playful, while Hazel's voice was merely sarcastic. Still, the familiarity was there.

"Hello, Hazel *Whitney* Grant," Grace greeted, smiling in a friendly sort of way. "I am glad that you finally

169

chose to emerge from your shell and talk to me." She studied Hazel's face to see how she felt about Grace's introduction.

Hazel smirked.

"Okay, you may not talk to me quite yet. I am glad you came out, though. I'm sure you will talk to me, and we'll get to be quite good friends."

Hazel remained silent, much to Grace's annoyance. Grace's biggest pet peeve was someone ignoring her, and this was a prime example. The frustrating girl just stared at Grace with a peculiar, taunting expression on her face.

Grace bit her lip. The girl was really getting on her nerves. Grace rarely got this worked up, but she was tired and ready to be home. She gritted her teeth and proclaimed, "I can tell that you're very independent."

"Very observant of you." Hazel snorted and tossed her head.

Grace decided to try a different tactic than the one that they had used with all of the other CLAIMED. "Do you have any friends? Any at all? I could be your friend—if you would let me, that is."

The girl—Hazel—patted the squirrel fondly. "Of course I have a friend. Iggy here is the best friend anyone could ever want."

Grace raised one eyebrow. "*Iggy?*"

"Ignis. It means fire in Latin. You know, for his color." The girl's voice dropped some its sarcasm as she gestured to the red squirrel. Her voice took on an enthusiastic tone instead. "He's my pal," she remarked simply.

This was the most that Hazel had said at one time so far in their conversation. Grace wanted to keep her talking, so she paused and pondered another question to ask the strange little girl. "Do you have any *human* friends?" she queried finally.

"Why would I want any? People just betray each other." Her voice was sarcastic again, and she spoke only briefly before lapsing back into silence.

Grace frowned. She decided that it was best to respond with another question, since this girl was full of questions and had no answers. She stuck to her original question. "So you've never had a *human* friend *at all*?"

Hazel glared. "What do you know about that?"

Grace stared at the girl in confusion. Hazel stared back defiantly. Grace spoke quickly and clearly, hoping that this time Hazel would answer the question without asking something else back. "What would you say if I told you that I want you to come with me?" she asked, breaking the ice.

"I would say *no*," Hazel responded without a second's hesitation. "Absolutely not. I shouldn't even really talk to you."

Grace frowned at the girl's response. Then she remembered. *The Initiation! I can't forget that, of all things!* She whipped out her hand, keeping the Magical words firmly in her mind. She touched Hazel's hand lightly and then rapidly jerked back, her mind reeling with shock and surprise.

Grace stood still. She had known that Hazel would feel the shock of electricity, but... She shook her mind to clear it, feeling dazed. She had not known that she would

171

feel it, too. She had not expected the electricity that had raced down her arm and through her fingertips into Hazel. She blinked and shook her hand, barely concealing a smile as she noticed that Hazel was wringing her hands, as well.

"Would you come with me now?" Grace grinned broadly. She did not blame Hazel for looking at her in a confused and slightly accusatory way.

Hazel analyzed the question. As usual, she responded with a query of her own. "You knew that would happen, didn't you? But what *is* it?"

Grace's grin did not waver as she answered the question. There was no reason to lie; she told the absolute truth. "Magic," she replied. The one word was more powerful than her trying to explain what had actually just happened.

"Magic..." Hazel's voice sounded dazed. "I would say you're crazy—that's an absolutely ridiculous answer—but it does make the most sense. And I really wish you'd stop grinning like that. It makes you look completely ridiculous." Hazel's tone was saucy and reprimanding, but not shocked.

"You didn't answer my question—are you coming back with me?" Grace persisted obstinately.

Hazel glared at Grace like she thought Grace had gone mad. Which, in Hazel's defense, was a perfectly reasonable assumption. She frowned. "You haven't told me anything at all about where you want to take me, though. That is a necessary bit of information." Hazel had stopped wringing her hands, and sarcasm had re-entered her voice, making her tone as slimy as a snake's would be—if snakes could talk.

Grace took a deep breath before plunging in. "A Magic School. I'm a Magician. You're a Magician. It only makes sense that we would be going to a Magic School. Plus," she added, "I'm sure the squirrel could come, too."

"Don't make fun of him," warned Hazel. "He understands more than you think. And you wouldn't want a squirrel for an enemy, now would you?"

Grace laughed. "I'm sure I wouldn't. But are you coming or not?" She stood quietly, awaiting the girl's answer. She wondered what Hazel was thinking. She hoped the girl's train of thought aided her own mission.

Hazel gave a clipped, short nod. "Alright, I'll come. I have to admit that life around here was getting pretty boring lately. I'm sure this Magic thing will bring much more adventure than sitting around here all day would." She lifted her chin haughtily. "I'll go, even though it means going along with *you.*"

Grace ignored the insult. She could have hugged Hazel for pure joy; she had been so afraid that the girl would not accept. *I am going home now*, she thought, her heart singing. "Oh, good," she breathed. "Then let's go."

Hazel held Ignis tightly as she followed Grace down the driveway to the road. She smirked at Grace, who was almost skipping with happiness. Grace was glad. She was *finally* going home!

Once they got to the main road, Grace grasped Hazel's hand firmly. She whispered the words of transportation under her breath, and the world disappeared into a tumbling mass of gray fuzz.

After about five seconds, the world popped into existence around the girls again. This time, though, Grace could sense the Magic in the air; it was as though she had become hyper-aware to it after her time away. She breathed deeply, allowing the refreshing air to flood through her body. A contented smile spread across her face.

Hazel looked at Grace. "Was that whirl of gray supposed to do anything?" she queried. "Because I don't think it worked."

Grace glanced down at the girl. "Oh, never mind that right now. Come on!" she urged, grinning all the while.

The two girls hurried onwards into the heart of New Yorin. After two hours of steady walking, they reached School Street, and Grace broke into a run. Hazel followed, clutching Ignis tightly.

Grace paused in front of the great marble structure. "The School of the CLAIMED," she announced, more to herself than to Hazel.

They walked up the sidewalk. They paused in front of the great door, waiting for it to open. It swung inside without a sound. The two girls stepped inside.

Grace blinked, taking in her surroundings. All of the CLAIMED were gathered in the hall, along with the Master and Jerra. The room was magnificently decorated with objects that vaguely reminded Grace of birthday party decorations from the other Dimension. She looked around in wonder. All of the people were grinning broadly.

"Surprise!" they yelled.

22. Grace's Surprise

Grace blinked. She wondered what could possibly be going on. Hazel stood beside her, feeling awkward.

"July twenty-ninth—it is your birthday, right?" asked Jerra, her smile faltering momentarily.

"Oh, right!" Grace nodded vigorously. "I had just lost track of the date…" She trailed off. "Thank you!" Grace stepped forward and embraced Jerra. Jerra stepped back after a moment and gestured towards the Master. Grace stared at the Master for a moment before she ran to her.

One tear rolled slowly down the Master's face. "I have missed you, child," she whispered.

When the Master released her, Grace grasped Hazel firmly by the hand. She gave the little girl a look of compassion. "This is Hazel Grant," she announced. "Hazel, this is everybody." She pointed to each person as she spoke. "Jerra, Tom, Dawn, Andrea, Michael, Zachariah, and the Master. The Master of Magic, that is."

Hazel nodded and offered a short wave. She seemed a little bit intimidated by the large group of people, but she was growing more confident every second. "And this—" Grace indicated to the squirrel that was perched on Hazel's shoulder "—is Ignis."

The Master smiled slightly, but it was not a teasing smile. "Hello, Hazel. This is our School. Jerra, would you please show Hazel to her room? I am sure I can make Ignis a bed soon, but for now he can sleep on a couple of towels on the floor. I trust this is satisfactory?"

Hazel nodded.

"Good," responded the Master. "And now, please, Jerra…"

"Of course," she replied. "Come along, Hazel. This will be your room." She led Hazel to the door next to Grace's own room. The two Magicians disappeared inside.

Grace smiled at her friends. Her heart brimmed with happiness, but she didn't know what to say. The Master saved her by speaking up. "Why don't you go put your bag down in your room, Grace? And then—we'll have a party."

Grace nodded quickly and hurried to her door. She grinned as it opened before her. It would take a while to get used to that again, but it was something that she was glad to re-adapt to. Quickly, she dropped her travel bag by the washstand. She splashed the cool, refreshing water over her face. Some of it trickled down her neck in cooling streams.

Finally, she dried her face and hands on the elegant towel that had been draped over the edge of the basin for her. She wondered who had thought to place it there for her. She withdrew a little hairbrush from her traveling bag. With a small sigh of happiness, she brushed her hair back smoothly before fastening it with a hair clip.

When she entered the hall once more, the room was filled with the chatter and laughter of all her friends. Jerra was talking with young Hazel, who seemed a little subdued by all of the people. Several other conversations were going on around the room, and Grace headed to the spot where Dawn and Andrea were talking with one another.

Andrea turned suddenly to Grace and embraced her. "I can't believe it's barely been a week since I last saw you!" she exclaimed. "I missed you so much, friend!"

Grace laughed, and the conversation continued.

The party lasted well into the evening. The friends played several games, and at one point the Master brought out an enormous birthday cake. Hazel felt rather left out at some points during the party, for she had never met any of the others. They did their best to include her in their conversations and games, and all of the children ended up enjoying themselves and the company of one another.

Grace could hardly process the fact that she was fourteen. It felt unreal, although she knew she would eventually get used to it.

The CLAIMED did not worry or even think about the destiny of the CLAIMED that night. They did not think about what mysteries might await them in the future. It seemed too far away, and the celebrations were much closer to home, as well as much more enjoyable.

As the night grew later, the children laughed and talked and played together, all Magic far from their minds. They were simply glad to be re-united and – more importantly – home.

Made in the USA
Middletown, DE
08 August 2018